PUSHKIN PRESS

Praise for
CHILDHOOD

'Profoundly unsettling and haunts the mind for long afterwards'
Sunday Times, Books of the Year

'These two posthumously published novellas by the Dutch writer Gerard Reve, skilfully translated by Sam Garrett, show he was capable of enormous and often unsettling power' **Observer**

'Enthralling… tales of the joys and pains of life that linger in the mind'
Financial Times

'Reve [has the ability]… to wring menace out of things left unsaid'
Daily Mail

'In a distinctive voice that captures childish incomprehension while still conveying what is missed by the still immature mind, the two works collected in *Childhood* are dark and even unpleasant, but both strong and impressive' **Asymptote Journal**

'I certainly can't find enough good things to say about *Childhood*… wonderfully evocative… Excellently translated by Sam Garrett, this is a gem of a book and highly recommended' **Shiny New Books**

'An incredibly compelling depiction of wartime' **Pendora Magazine**

Praise for
THE EVENINGS

A BOOK OF THE YEAR
in the *Observer*, *Financial Times* and *Irish Times*

'A masterpiece… What can I say that will put this book where it belongs, in readers' hands and minds?' **Tim Parks, Guardian**

'A master[   ] youthful
malaise [   ] sh Times

GERARD REVE (1923–2006) is considered one of the greatest postwar Dutch authors, and was also one of the first openly gay writers in the country's history. A complicated and controversial character, Reve is also hugely popular and critically acclaimed. His 1947 debut *The Evenings* was ranked as the best Dutch novel of the twentieth century by the Society of Dutch literature and was a three-time book of the year when it was first published in English in 2016. The two novellas that make up *Childhood* were first published in Dutch in 1949 and 1950. This is the first time they have been translated into English.

SAM GARRETT has translated some 40 novels and works of nonfiction, including *The Evenings* by Gerard Reve. He has won prizes and appeared on shortlists for some of the world's most prestigious literary awards, and is the only translator to have twice won the British Society of Authors' Vondel Prize for Dutch–English translation.

GERARD REVE

CHILDHOOD

Two Novellas

Translated from the Dutch
by Sam Garrett

PUSHKIN PRESS
LONDON

Pushkin Press
71–75 Shelton Street
London WC2H 9JQ

Original text © 1949 Erven Gerard Reve
Published with De Bezige Bij, Amsterdam
English translation © Sam Garrett 2018

Werther Nieland was first published as *Werther Nieland*, 1949

The Fall of the Boslowits Family was first published as
De ondergang van de familie Boslowits, 1950

First published by Pushkin Press in 2018

N **ederlands**
letterenfonds
dutch foundation
for literature

The publisher gratefully acknowledges the support
of the Dutch Foundation for Literature

1 3 5 7 9 8 6 4 2

ISBN 13: 978-1-78227-459-9

Designed and typeset by Tetragon, London
Printed in Great Britain by the CPI Group, UK

www.pushkinpress.com

CONTENTS

WERTHER NIELAND

O N A WEDNESDAY AFTERNOON in December, when the weather was dark, I tried to wrench a drainpipe off the back of the house; this without success. Then I took up a hammer and pulverized a few thin twigs from the currant bush atop a post in the garden fence. The weather remained dark.

I could think of nothing else to do and went to see Dirk Heuvelberg. (Dirk had, for as far as my memory reached, lived beside us. At the age of four he still had not learned to speak; until the age of three he walked on all fours. I also remember how, when we were little, he would come scrambling to our kitchen door: he heralded his arrival with great shrieks. When requested to do so, he would eat horse manure from the pavement. Later, he retained the ability to move quickly on his hands and feet and continued to speak with no little difficulty. He liked to claim, with a certain pride, that his tongue was too long and too loosely attached; to support this claim, he would clack it loudly. On that December afternoon as well, in the back room of his house, he spoke awkwardly and unclearly still, his words bursting and stumbling from his lips. He had remained small. I was eleven at the time.)

A pale, sallow-skinned boy was playing at Dirk's—one I had never seen before. Standing by the window, he greeted me falteringly. "He's Werther Nieland," Dirk said. From a box of Meccano on the floor they were building a hoist, which they hoped to power by means of a windmill, but they had not started on that part yet.

"You'd be better off building the windmill first," I said. "That's much more important. You need to know how much power it has before you can figure out how to build the hoist. And whether you need to use a large pulley or a small one. And then of course," I went on, "you need to pick someone to supervise the construction. Preferably someone who lives, for example, beside the house with the windmill, or close to it." I spoke this final sentence under my breath, too quietly for them to hear. A brief silence filled the lightless little room. (The wallpaper was a dark brown, all the woodwork was painted dark green and the windows were covered in crocheted curtains the colour of terracotta.)

As the silence wore on, I eyed the new boy. He was thin and spindly and a little taller than me. His expression was detached and bored, his lips moist and puffy. He had dark, deep-set eyes, black curls and a low forehead. The skin on his face was blemished and flaky. I felt the urge to in some way torment him or inflict pain on him underhandedly. "Don't you agree, Werther, that we should build the windmill first?" I asked. "Yes, of course," he replied diffidently, without meeting my gaze. "He's a sweet-toothed little creature," I said to myself, "I know that for a fact." While Dirk was busy bolting something into place, the two of us looked out of the window at the tilled garden; atop the bare soil lay an old washtub and a couple of weathered planks. A haze of moisture and settling smoke hung between the rooftops. I moved up close to Werther and, without either of them seeing it, feigned punches at his back.

Although Dirk too was in agreement with my proposal concerning the windmill, we still did not set about building it right away, but remained sitting together, doing nothing. "Of course, you two don't have to build a windmill, not if you don't feel like it," I said. "But that would be rather silly, for you could learn a great deal from it." Outside, daylight was beginning to fade. "Listen, Werther," I said. "Is your house in a very windy spot?" He did not reply. "Then I could come and help you." I went on: "Then we could build a windmill you can use to operate machines in the kitchen. It would be no problem at all, I have time enough. And making a promise and not keeping it, I would never do that." I was intent on finding ways to visit him at home.

Werther did not respond to my words; perhaps I was not speaking loudly enough, or perhaps it was the faint music coming from a radio somewhere at the front of the house.

Afternoon was drawing to a close by the time the three of us went outside to saunter along the pavements. The street lights were already lit. Werther announced that it was time for him to go home; we accompanied him all the way. He lived on the top floors of a detached house, on a corner beyond which there were no more buildings, only a view of broad fields stretching out along the dyke.

"Oh yes," I said loudly, "when the wind is blowing it's quite strong here: I can tell that right away. Does your house have a balcony?" Werther, however, invited neither of us to come up. When he had already reached the doorway, I went up and asked him hastily, so that Dirk couldn't hear, when I could come to make the windmill.

"Boys are allowed to come on Saturday afternoon," he said, closing the door behind him.

Arriving home, I first went to reflect in the garden storage shed, where I kept my secret documents. There, in pencil on an old piece of packing paper, I wrote: "There will be a club. Important messages have been sent already. If anybody wants to ruin it, he will be punished. On Sunday, Werther Nieland is going to join." I tucked the paper away beneath a crate, along with other scraps of writing.

That same evening, in the kitchen, I found a wide vase of clear glass devoid of ridges or curves: a round aquarium, in fact; from then on, I was allowed to use it as such. After school the next day I caught some sticklebacks and, rather than tossing them into hedges, sewer drains or onto the paving stones as had been my custom, I placed them in my aquarium. I peered at them through the glass, which seemed to magnify them slightly. But I tired of this soon enough. Scooping them out one by one, I cut off their heads with a paring knife. "These are the beheadings," I said quietly, "for you are all the dangerous kings of the water." For the proceedings I had chosen a sheltered spot in the garden, out of sight of any spies. I dug a shallow hole and carefully buried the dead creatures in it, their heads back in place now and all in a row; for the interment I sprinkled petals from the old, wilted tulips I had taken from the table in the parlour.

Then I returned to the canal for a second catch. It looked as though rain would fall on the way home, but none did. Back in the garden again I suddenly found the lopping-off of heads to be a laborious and time-consuming task. From Meccano I therefore began to build a chopping machine, to which I planned to attach a razor blade; it was at that point, however, that calamity struck.

While attaching the razor my left hand slipped and my index finger slid with force along the blade: the cut ran from fingertip to past the knuckle; the wound was deep and bled heavily. Feeling dizzy and nauseous, I went inside.

My mother dressed the wound. "It was a razor blade," I said plaintively. "I wasn't even playing with it: I wanted to make something with it." I knew that the little creatures, who told each other everything after all, had sent the accident my way.

"Now be careful with it," my mother said. "Don't go outside any more, not while it's so cold. You remember what happened to Spaander, don't you?"

(Spaander was an acquaintance who had once suffered a similar injury. He lived on Vrolikstraat and made a living by sharpening knives and scissors from a handcart he pushed around town. Once, while sharpening a blade on the street, he cut his thumb. It was very cold, the

14

soaked bandage hardened and, without him noticing, the thumb froze, so that the top half had to be amputated. My mother always told this story in great detail, and whenever she did she would explain as a bonus, although apropos of nothing, that Spaander's son had studied for his teaching certificate in the only room their dwelling possessed and—and this was impressed on me each time—without allowing himself to be distracted by the voices around him. "You see, now that is gumption," she would say then. Even if our house had had ten rooms, I knew, I would never learn a thing. Every time old Spaander came by, I was allowed to view and touch the stump of his thumb. "He has a very stupid wife," my mother said often. Each time anew she would tell us that, due to some internal collapse, the woman had developed a huge sagging waist for which she was prescribed a medical corset. She went out to work each day, and the corset got in her way, so after the first day she never wore it again. "When she's down scrubbing the floor, her paunch hangs all the way to the ground," my mother would say. "And the good woman is only thirty-four years old. Isn't that horrific?")

The accident with the thumb she now revisited in great detail. "Whatever you do, you mustn't go out in the cold," she repeated emphatically. When the first light frost came, she even wanted me to stay inside at the weekend. But at last a solution was found: she fashioned for me a sheath of light-blue flannel to wear on top of the bandage, with two cords bound round the wrist. Now I could spend hours in the garden again.

I did not finish the chopping machine: I took the parts, wrapped them in newspaper and hid them away in the storage shed. The water in the glass vase had frozen; the fish floated rigidly in the middle, close to the surface, inside the clump of ice; the vase itself had cracked. I examined the fish closely. "They're wizards," I said out loud. "You can't fool me." I buried the vase and everything in it as deeply as I could. "They can't rise to the surface now, not any more," I thought. Saturday was already upon us.

That afternoon I made my way to Werther's. There was a touch of frost in the air, but no wind. I did not ring the bell right away but remained standing in the entranceway, examining the door. It was painted green, and above the nameplate reading "J. Nieland" was a round, enamelled sign with a green, five-pointed star, encircled by the words *Esperanto Parolata*. I listened at the letter box but heard only a hissing silence. The draught of air that brushed my face carried with it a vague, indeterminate odour, unlike anything I had smelled before, I thought; it reminded me of new curtains, matting or upholstery, but with an unfamiliar note. "This odour is made by magic and kept in a bottle," I said to myself. I rang the bell.

The latch clicked, the door opened. A large woman with a broad, pale face was standing at the top of the stairs; she did not speak a word or ask me my business. "Today is Saturday afternoon," I shouted up, "and I was allowed to come then. I'm here for Werther." The woman did not move, only nodded. I climbed the stairs. When I got to the top she still said nothing, only stared at me curiously.

She had a strange look about her. The mouth in her wrinkled, oldish face seemed incapable of closing completely; her coarse yellow teeth remained visible all the time. She had beady eyes like a hen or a pigeon: they peered at me from deep in their sockets and shifted almost imperceptibly. The crown of her head was ringed with drab, fluffy hair.

"I'm Werther's mother," she said suddenly, then smiled and took a few pattering, dance-like steps across the floor; I thought for a moment that she had stumbled, but that could not have been the case. The light on the landing, onto which two doors with yellow frosted glass gave out, was dim. For a moment I imagined that the house's odour had been specially concocted in order to stun me and lock me up in a box.

"You've hurt your finger, I see," she said. "Well, I'll be careful when I take your coat." While she was helping me, she made those strange little pattering moves again. "Who are you anyway?" she asked. "One of Werther's little friends?" She placed her hand heavily on the back of my neck. "I'm Elmer, I was allowed to come over this afternoon, that's what Werther said," I croaked. There was no way I could flee back down the stairs, for Werther's mother was blocking them now.

"Oh, is that what Werther said?" she asked. "I'm always the last to know, now aren't I? You're such naughty little boys. Are you naughty too, sometimes?" "I don't know," I said quietly. "You don't, do you?" she asked. She took hold of my shoulders as she spoke, squeezed them and smacked me a few times softly on the bottom. Then she pushed me out in front of her into the kitchen.

Werther was standing there, looking through the glass of the door onto the balcony. He was holding a fork, eating pickled mussels from a saucer. "I'm Elmer, you remember me, I said I'd come over," I hastened to say. "We had to build that windmill."

The kitchen was almost bare. It contained only a little wooden table.

Without answering, Werther went on jabbing at the mussels and stuffing them into his mouth. "The tastiest bits are the little trunks," he said then, holding up a mussel with its pale, stringy appendage. "I always save those for last."

"Is his little trunk the tastiest?" asked his mother, who was still standing in the kitchen doorway. "And do you eat that up? How cruel of you. How would you like it if I ate the tastiest part of you?" She grinned and snorted loudly. Werther stared at her for a moment, then began to giggle.

Werther's mother handed me a fork. "Take some too, if you like," she said. "You can even pull off the trunk, if it doesn't appeal to you." Werther laughed loudly at that. I jabbed my fork into a mussel, but as I raised it quickly to my mouth I gave the fork a turn, to keep the little tendril from dangling. The flavour did not appeal to me, however, and I limited myself to fishing a few little pieces of pickled onion from the saucer. His mother kept an eye on my every move.

"Werther, we need to get started on that windmill," I said, for I wanted to go out onto the balcony. He did not reply. "If someone happens to come by who is good at building windmills, you should take advantage of it," I went on. "So it would be silly not to get started. A person who knows a lot about windmills should be made the leader right away." I spoke quietly, because his mother was listening. Werther asked her whether we could go to work on the balcony.

"Out of the question," she said gruffly. "I don't want any hammering and making a mess out there, with all that filth you two track in with you."

"We may just do it anyway, once you leave the kitchen," Werther said. "Oh, is that so?" she asked. "Then you may just have to be punished again, in your birthday suit. And your cute little friend along with you." Werther showed the start of a smile, but then lowered his eyes. His mother took a step in my direction and said loudly: "Elmer," (I was amazed that she remembered my name) "they're such ruffians: absolute bandits is what they are."

She took a sheet of dirty white cardboard, which looked like the backing from an old block-calendar, from the mantelpiece, turned it over and began deciphering the text written there in pen. "Back then, a good five years ago now, I wrote down the things they did, every once in a while," she said. Then she started reading aloud:

"While in the kitchen, I hear Werther in the garden. My oh my. He's out there with Martha. He's on the swing. Then she wants to get on, and as soon as she's sitting on it, he wants to get back on again. What a terrible tease!"

"We were living in Tuindorp Oostzaan at the time," she said by way of an aside. "Have you ever been there?"

"No, I've never been there, but I know where it is," I said cautiously. She resumed her reading.

"There is snow everywhere, so no shortage of tomfoolery. Werther is the stronger of the two, for Martha gets most of the snow down her neck. She gets the worst of it. I am standing in the kitchen and I see everything, even though they don't realize. Really, I can see everything. Even if they don't think so, the rascals."

She must have been short-sighted, for now she held the sheet of cardboard close to her eyes. Running her gaze down over the rest, she went on:

"Now it is summer. Everything is growing and flowering. Werther has gone with Martha to the swimming pool. Yesterday, in the bedroom, they practised on dry land. He has a new pair of swimming trunks, blue ones. Oh, how proud he is!"

Here, it seemed, the text ended. A silence fell. Werther looked outside. His mother returned the sheet of cardboard to its place, stood there for a moment and suddenly said: "I enjoyed writing that down. It's handy, because you can go back and read it later on."

"How long ago was that, exactly?" I asked. "About five years ago," she replied.

"Yes," I said, "but isn't there a day or a date on it?" "No," she said, "it was just for fun, of course. Not long ago someone said it was good that I'd written that down.

Who was that again, Werther?" He thought about it. None of us moved.

"Come, let's go inside," she said then. She bustled us out in front of her, into the adjoining room; it contained nothing but a table with a ping-pong net and four benches. I remained standing warily, not knowing whether I was allowed to walk through to the room on the street side, the sliding doors to which stood ajar. Just then, however, we were beckoned by a little man who was sitting with his back to us in a red velvet armchair. It was Werther's father.

Until he moved, I had not noticed that he was there. "You boys are welcome to sit in here, Werther," he said, "as long as you're a bit careful what you do." His lined face was pasty and sallow, his eyebrows slanted downwards at the corners. The grey eyes beneath them bore a look that was weary or sorrowful. When he spoke he spoke reluctantly, as though the effort tired him. His shoulders were narrow. Thinking about it, I decided he must be smaller than Werther's mother.

From the looks of it he was simply sitting there, thinking, for he was not smoking and there were no books or newspapers on the round table in front of him. I didn't know whether to shake his hand, and so I shuffled my feet awkwardly a few times, then sat down in one of the armchairs. Werther took a seat by the window.

Although the room we had come through was almost bare (there lay only a thin mat on the floor), this one was filled to overflowing: it contained no fewer than six end tables with lace doilies, tabourets and hassocks; crocheted cushions had been tossed wherever space allowed. The dark wallpaper had a pattern of large, brown autumn leaves. There were eight hanging lamps: two metal ones, two with jigsawed shades in the shape of a pointed cap and four cylindrical lamps with parchment shades painted with the images of sailing ships. Atop the mantelpiece above the lit hearth, between three gnomes, a shepherd girl and a porcelain toadstool, stood a copper statuette of a naked worker with a hammer slung over his shoulder; the doily on which it rested fluttered in the heat. "Don't you two go making scratches on the armrests with your nails," Werther's mother said before turning and going back to the kitchen.

"Are you a schoolmate of Werther's?" his father asked. "No," I answered, "I'm a friend, I think." At that moment the sun broke through, casting hard light on his face and thin neck, which proved also to be covered in wrinkles. Amid the hair on the top of his skull, a thin spot became visible, where the skin looked crusty and raw. The sight of it made me feel hatred and pity, at one and the same time.

Werther stepped away from the window. "When I'm finished with school, I'm going to the literary-economic polytechnic," he said. "What kinds of things do they teach you there again, Father?"

"Lots of foreign languages," his father replied. "Mostly languages." "And what kinds of languages?" Werther went on. "French, German and English," the man answered tersely. His hands fluttered at the sides of his chair, as though he were fighting the urge to pluck at the upholstery. The leather uppers of his shoes, I saw, had separated from the soles along the instep.

"But no Esperanto?" Werther asked. His father merely shook his head.

"What kind of language is that, anyway?" I asked, addressing myself partly to Werther, partly to his father. "Do you really want to know or are you only curious?" the man asked. "If you're truly interested, I'll explain it to you." "Yes, I would very much like to know," I said.

He glanced at me again, hesitantly. "In the last century," he said then, "in 1887 to be precise, a big, big man—and I don't mean big in the sense of size, I mean big as in extraordinary, learned—made that language from a lot of other languages. Werther, you know who that was."

"Zadelhoff," Werther said. "Dr Zamenhof," his father corrected him. "Ludwig Lazarus Zamenhof. If you're interested, I can tell you a great deal more about him. He lived in Bialystok, in Russian Poland. People there spoke four or five different languages. And he decided to put an end to that confusion and then he created Esperanto, the international language. He took something from each language. 'And' is *kai*, there's an example for you. *Kai* is from the Greek. That's how he did it."

"That sign with the star on it, on the door, that's what it's about," said Werther.

"If someone from a foreign country comes here and they have learned Esperanto, then we can speak with each other and understand each other," his father went on. "That is the great work Dr Zamenhof did." He was silent for a moment.

"But there are always too few people willing to work together," he said now, pensively and speaking more to himself. "I often run into acquaintances who ask me about it. But when I tell them: you should learn the language, they don't do it. They say it's too difficult to learn all those words."

He let his hands dangle between his knees and stared at the carpet. "Would you like to learn it?" he asked suddenly. "I don't know," I replied. "I don't know whether I'd be able." "You wouldn't have to start right away," he said, "but if I were to give you a brochure—that's sort of a little book—you'd be able to understand it, wouldn't

25

you?" "I don't know," I said. "It's not in Esperanto," he pushed on, "but it explains how Dr Zamenhof came up with it. It's quite fascinating. I'll give you one later on, but will you promise to bring it back? Otherwise it costs money, if people buy it, fifteen cents." It seemed as though he were about to get up and fetch one, but he remained seated.

"We're going to play ping-pong," Werther said. He led me to the room we had come through, where he extended the leaves on the table and took bats and a ball from a wooden box. "I've never played this before," I said. He explained the rules, but I listened only half-heartedly and peered out of the window from the corner of my eye. On a balcony on the far side of the courtyard, a large German shepherd dog was pacing back and forth; occasionally it barked and stuck its head through the bars, got stuck and then pulled it back with a yelp. The animal, it occurred to me, could go nowhere, not even jump the railing, for it had no room to make a running start.

We began the game. Werther's father remained seated in just the way we had found him.

After we had played for a while, his mother came in from the kitchen. She stood beside the table and followed the ball with her eyes. After she had done this for a while, she began snatching at the ball, barely missing it each time. "Mother, you're ruining our game," Werther said. His mother pulled her hand back immediately and stared at him. "You look nice, when you play so energetically," she said; "you're a very handsome boy. Or should I say, a very handsome young man." At these words, Werther stopped swinging the bat and glanced quickly at his father in the front room. He was still sitting there, motionlessly, with his back to us. The ball hit the floor behind Werther. His mother snatched it up quickly and pretended to run away with it. At Werther's insistence, however, she put it back on the table.

"I like that kind of thing," she said to me. "I'm just as fond of fun and games as you are. When we used to play out on the street, you should have seen how silly we were! Did you think we weren't? If there was one thing I couldn't get enough of, it was having fun. Mentally I'm very youthful, you know."

She took the bat away from me and stood in my place. "Now it's me against you, Werther," she said. She made rapid little shaking motions with her upper body, as though in time to some music we couldn't hear.

They began to play. After she had missed the ball four times she tossed the bat, even though the game was not yet finished, onto the table. "Werther is the champion," she said; "congratulations." She walked over to him with her hand held out, but when he went to shake it she feinted, reached past his hand and quickly grabbed his crotch. He giggled and sprang away from her. "You're my fine little Werther," she said. His leap had brought him to the sliding doors, and he looked at his father. The man turned his head. "Did any of you hear that?" he asked. "What, Father?" Werther asked in a frightened voice. "I didn't hear anything."

A brief silence fell. Werther's mother picked up the bat and swung it enthusiastically back and forth, as though she were conducting music. I looked at the floor. "The box is going to be opened," I thought.

From outside came a sort of bellowing, a rising and falling tone. For a moment I thought it was a sort of foghorn, but then realized it could only be a voice. "It's out in front here, on the street," said Werther's father. He stood up. We all went to the window.

Standing on the pavement beside the stretch of parkland was a thin man in a dark-green, furry coat. His craggy face was grim and weathered. In his right hand he held a large tin horn: a megaphone, I knew it was called. Just when we had all moved up to the window, he raised it to his lips and produced a long, deep call that sounded like "Hue!" This was followed immediately by a shout: "The war is coming. Be on your guard!" Then, moving at a brisk pace, he disappeared around the corner.

I did not know whether to laugh or maintain a mournful silence.

I did, however, realize that it must be impossible to understand everything that happened, that there were things that remained a mystery and caused a mist of fear to come rolling in.

"That was crazy old Verfhuis," said Werther. "He lives on Onderlangs." His mother shook her head pityingly. "It's a morbid disposition," she said, "a morbid disposition." Werther's father said nothing and went back to his chair. I was overtaken by the grave fear that he would now go looking for the booklet (I believed that he would read to me aloud from it and, if I did not understand, that he would stuff me into a barrel or a sack).

"We need to go to the kitchen," I said quietly to Werther. "I need to speak to you alone, quite urgently." We made our way there. The kitchen was silent; the only sound was from the gas flame hissing quietly beneath the kettle. From outside, almost no noise made its way in either.

"I have made a number of discoveries," I said. "I can confide in you about them. If you go home with me now, right away, I can show you things that are extremely important. I also have a tomb at home, a real one." I longed to leave his house as quickly as possible.

29

He agreed to go, but first he wanted to tell his parents that he was leaving.

"You can't do that," I said with great insistence. "It's a secret. Enemies might find out and follow us."

We descended the stairs without a sound and raced off. When we got to my house, we first wandered about the garden for a bit. The faintest breath of wind caused an almost noiseless rustling in the bushes. We hung by our arms from a branch of the laburnum till it broke, then planted the branch upright in the ground. Werther asked where the tomb was. I took him along to the storage shed, where we sat down on an old mat and hung a gunny sack before the entrance, so that no one could look in. "This is the Tomb of Deepest Death," I said. Werther said nothing and peered listlessly into the half-light. "We have to set up the club," I said. "Then we can dig the tombs. Because they are badly needed."

Suddenly I recalled that, the day before, I had found a dead starling and secreted it beneath some leaves in a corner of the garden. "We have to go outside now," I said, "the ceremony is about to begin." After we found the dead bird, I built a pyre of wood. On it I burned the body, from which bubbling brown juices seethed. The charred, peculiar-smelling lump that remained I placed in a boat-shaped box that had once held dates. In the mound of earth that I threw together quickly then, I dug a tunnel with no outlet, and fortified the walls of it with planks: into this I shoved the little box; after sealing the entrance, I sprinkled the top of the mound with fine ashes from the fire. "The secret bird has gone to earth," I sang to myself. I repeated the sentence in my mind, over and over, but did not dare to speak it aloud.

"Now we have to set up the club," I said again. "If we wait too long, enemy clubs will be set up too, I'm sure you're aware of that." I had him follow me to the storage shed again, where I now lit a candle. Then I wrote our names in an old pocket diary, which I produced from beneath the crate. "Now the club exists," I said after reading our names aloud slowly. "It's called the Club For The Tombs, the C.F.T.T. Everyone who is a member, in their garden we can make a tomb. That is very important."

"I'm sure you understand," I went on, "that someone has to be the boss: someone who says, for example, when there is going to be a meeting. It is best if that someone is someone at whose house the club was set up." Werther nodded, but I did not believe he was listening carefully. I stood up and leaned against the wall.

"I am the president," I said, "that has already been written. You are the secretary, but that must remain a secret. You will be the secretary, of course, but the president does everything that needs to be done: that's always the way it goes." Werther asked if the only thing the club did was make tombs.

"The club members also make windmills," I said. "That has a lot to do with tombs, as I'm sure you understand. Because the one who can make a tomb, who came up with the idea first, is also the boss over the windmills. If anyone tries to ruin the club, his dick will be cut off. Now I'll tell you precisely what kind of club it's going to be."

I had no idea, however, how to go on. I searched around and found some old shoelaces, divided them up and set them on fire. After putting out the flames, we breathed the odour they spread as they smouldered. I extinguished the candle as well, so that by waving our arms in the dark we could make fiery stripes and circles that gave off a faint, purplish light; for quite some time we remained sitting like that, sunk in thought. "We should go to the sand," Werther said. He went to fetch Dirk.

The three of us set off walking.

By the time we got to the sandy flats beyond the dyke the wind was blowing a bit harder, occasionally throwing up little clouds of dust. As we moved on we jumped in and out of hollows, searching as we did for objects the builders might have left behind, but never found anything other than a paltry plank or half-buried newspaper.

When we came to a sandpit that was particularly large and deep, I asked them to sit down in it with me. The cold wind tossed a flurry of sand in our hair. "This is the first meeting of the club," I said. "The president is going to give a speech." I paused for a moment. "Dirk, you need to say something now and then hand over the floor to me," I said, "because you're the deputy secretary." But he said nothing, only plucked at the roots of a grassy plant. A dusting of sand blew in our faces again. "You can become the deputy secretary," I went on, "I can see to that. It has to remain a secret, of course, because the president does everything that needs to be done. Now you have to hand over the floor to the president." He remained silent. I addressed my request to Werther this time. "Elmer, give your speech," he said.

I stood up and began: "Respected members. The club has been set up. It is called the C.F.T.T. So there is a club, but we're not nearly there yet. It must not be a club of which we are merely members: it must be a club that is on the march. What we don't need are members on paper only. Members who, when their president asks them to say something, don't. They are no use to us. They would be better off getting up and leaving."

"We should go pull down a tree over there," Dirk said, pointing over his shoulder to the little park behind him. He drew a long, sturdy rope from his pocket.

"You're an enemy of the club," I said. "You should be tied up." We caught him, tossed the loop that was already in the rope around his ankles and dragged him around the pit. In a whimpering voice, he begged us to let him go. Instead, we climbed out of the pit and pulled him up over the edge. The rope was cutting into his skin, and he now began crying loudly, so that we let go of him and ran away. When we saw that he was not coming after us, we slowed to a walk and continued across the bare flats.

"It's his own fault," I said. "He wants to ruin the club because he's the spy; that happens often: that someone acts at first like they want to join and then goes and tells the enemy everything."

We came to the swampy stretch of ground that we called "the wilderness". Here, in a shallow, brownish rivulet that seemed to well up from the ground and ran through a stand of reeds into a ditch, we built a dam of stones, creating a dirty waterfall. Then we broke the dam apart and, hiding ourselves amid the elderberry bushes, tossed the stones at flocks of sparrows until we hit one. It was impossible to tell who had made the throw. The animal appeared to have been crushed, but when Werther pushed the stone aside, it shivered weakly. We stood looking at it pensively. "This is the secret bird from the spy club," I said, "because they've set that up. They're so mean: they don't dare to do anything themselves and they send birds to pick up letters."

We remained waiting for the bird to die so that we could take it with us to burn, but it did not stop its movements. Finally, I built a pyre of dry reeds and asked Werther to place the animal on top. "This is the punishment for spying on our club while we're building waterfalls," I said once Werther had complied. I lit the reeds, but the fire kept going out. Finally, my matches were finished and we left the smouldering pile behind. Dusk was falling. We walked on without a word, downcast.

Close to his house we entered a small grocer's where Werther wanted to buy some liquorice. I intended to wait outside, but he urged me to come in. The shop was dark and smelled of wet soil.

While we were waiting for someone to arrive from the back, I became convinced that there must be a trapdoor hidden behind the counter, granting access to a vast underground chamber. That was where the earth creatures lived and crept amid the tree roots that served as their pillars. Without Werther seeing it,

I held on tightly to a rail that ran along the counter, so that I would not unexpectedly, without a struggle, be dragged down through the floor.

Finally, a pale little woman with grey hair came from the back and began counting out liquorice drops. "Ma'am, could I ask you something?" Werther said suddenly in a slow, sluggish voice. "How do they make liquorice drops, anyway?" The woman said she did not know.

"Liquorice is made from a special kind of flour," I said. "And from herbs that grow underneath trees: those are the main things, because there's only a little bit of flour in them." In fact, I knew nothing about how liquorice was made. "I think it's weird," I went on, "that you don't even know that. You are actually rather stupid."

When we were outside again, I said: "If you know about a lot of things, you can stay in the club. Otherwise you have to get out. Because members who are stupid are no use to us." We sucked on the liquorice drops and ambled along with no clear plan. "We have to make sure it's a good club," I said dully.

We arrived at the shelter at the end of the bus route. Here we sat shivering on the mud floor and remained silent for a time. Finally, just to have something to say, I asked him how old his sister was. I had not yet seen her. "She's nearly nine," he said. The wind had picked up a bit and soughed along the wooden walls.

"I have a brother and he ran away from home," I said. "He's on a ship." When I had ascertained that Werther was listening, I went on: "He's the same age as me." Now Werther asked why he had run away.

"That's a long story," I replied, "and a sad one too." I paused for a moment.

"I've never told anyone else," I continued, "so I'll tell you, but you mustn't tell anyone else." He promised. "All right," I said, "but if I tell you and you give it away, then you'll be cut dead, do you understand?" He nodded. "It's actually too late to tell you the whole thing," I said, "for afternoon is drawing to a close: darkness is making its approach." (These last twelve words I remembered having read somewhere.)

"That brother was a horrible bastard," I started in, "because he always acted mean. He cut the heads off fish. And then my mother locked him in the cellar. When it got dark, he climbed out of the window. He took almost nothing with him, only his blankets from his bed."

I waited for a moment, then added: "Do you think I enjoy talking about this? If you do, you're mistaken. It's a terrible thing. That's why I'm so sad this afternoon. Do you know what his name is?"

Again, I paused. I could not come up with a name right away. "His name is André," I said then. "And the ship is called *Godspeed*: that means they sail straight ahead." (I had seen the name once on a sand barge.) "He's sailing on the other side of the world now, but when he comes home he's bringing an animal with him, and it's for me."

A bus driver came in and chased us out of the shelter. We strolled in the direction of my house. "André brought me a parrot once too," I said, "that he bought somewhere. And it mimicked everything you said. But it died. All animals die in the end."

When we got to my house, I invited him to go to the storage shed again. "There's going to be a big, festive club meeting at my house," I said. "We need to talk about that." Once we were seated on the mat, once the gunny sack was drawn and I had lit the candle again, I said: "It is truly horrible, what happened with my brother, but a person shouldn't be sad all the time. That's why the club is holding a festive gathering at my house tomorrow. I'm going to put together a tremendous programme. Make sure you're on time: otherwise there's a chance that you'll get there and it will already have started. I'll give a big speech."

"Can I bring Martha?" he asked. "Yes, I suppose you can," I said slowly, sounding grave. "We could always make her a prospective member. Later, she can become a real one."

Silence seeped in; our arms and legs were growing stiff from the cold. "I'll show you a picture of that brother," I said, and asked him to wait right there.

In the parlour, where the evening shadows had fallen, my mother was napping by the window. I carefully took the frame, which contained a multitude of little photos behind glass, down from the wall. In doing so I bumped lightly against the two blown eggs that hung on thin wires either side of it. (This was a big, white ostrich egg and a smaller, black egg from an emu. Whenever there was horseplay going on or we were throwing things around the room, my mother would shout: "Look out for the ostrich egg! Look out for the emu egg!")

On my way back to the storage shed, I picked out a small photo of a barefoot boy beside a big dog, taken in some kind of park. (I had no idea who it was.) "This is André," I said, "this is that brother who has caused me such sorrow, and still does." Werther examined the photograph closely, but then began looking at the others too. "Those have nothing to do with it!" I said, snatching the frame roughly from his hands. In doing so I bumped it against the doorpost and chipped a corner of the glass. I said nothing and took the photos back to where they came from, in the same stealthy fashion.

As he was leaving, Werther announced that he would come to the meeting the next day. I walked with him no further than the exit to the garden and mumbled a farewell.

Before dinner time I used the mat from the shed to build a tent at the garden's edge, against one wall of the neighbours' bicycle shed; on the ground in the middle of it I planted a heavy concrete paving stone.

"This is the centre of the temple," I said quietly. Sunk in my musings, I set an old, cracked iron casserole atop the paving stone and built in it a little fire of twigs. It produced a huge cloud of smoke. I took the blue cover I had torn from an old notebook, smoothed out the wrinkles and, after sitting down in the tent, wrote on it in chalk: "To André, who is a brother. On the ship, so On Board. They have to give him this letter." I rolled up the paper and tossed it into the flames.

Then something peculiar happened: footsteps approached in the neighbouring garden and stopped just outside the tent. I placed the metal lid on the pan. There was the sound of muttering, followed immediately by someone tossing a bucket of water over the tent. I remained deathly still, without a sound. The water did not get inside but poured loudly off the tent. Then the footsteps moved away, a latch rattled and a door closed. It seemed possible to me that the tossing of the letter into the fire and the rush of water were magically connected, but I could not fathom how. When my mother called me to dinner, I remained seated and shivered. "He stinks," my brother said when I arrived at the table at last, "like a tough kipper. He does all kinds of filthy things. It has to be filthy, otherwise he won't do it."

The next day I spent decorating our bedroom. I tacked the branches of old Christmas trees (brought in from the street) to the walls and wove lengths of white crêpe paper through them. Then I began installing the wires for the lighting.

Quite some time before, in a bicycle shop, I had succeeded in purchasing a bell transformer for sixty cents but had not been allowed to use it: my mother did not trust the thing. Now I received permission, on condition that I show it first to a neighbourhood acquaintance, a little hunchbacked tailor they called the Rabbi: he had a reputation for being knowledgeable when it came to electricity. "Yes, that's a normal transformer," he said immediately, but he kept me for a long time as he explained how to connect the poles, even though that was indicated clearly on the Bakelite cover. His wife, who was wracked with rheumatism and could barely move her swollen fingers, looked at the contraption short-sightedly and said: "You don't want to be fooling around with those things."

Her husband asked whether I knew that there were people who removed the covers from wall sockets and held their fingers against the contacts, just for fun.

Then he went on to tell me what had happened to him a few days earlier. In his workshop, which looked out on the garden, he had hung up all kinds of loose wiring, running across the ceiling like clothes lines. That afternoon, as he was standing at his bench to cut cloth, he held up the material to get a better look and snipped through the wire running to the lamp. An explosion and a flash followed, he received a bad shock and it caused a short circuit in the house. Neighbours who were in the next garden had hurried over, and later described the effect they had seen as a "blue jet of fire". He was convinced that a layer of worn lacquer on the handles of the shears was all that had kept him from being killed.

When I got home I installed the transformer and hooked it to three bicycle-lamp bulbs, which I tucked in amid the pine boughs. In crayon, on a piece of cardboard, I wrote "Join the C.F.T.T" and hung it among the greenery. Finally, I turned on the electricity. Then I asked my father to come and look.

With one hand in his pocket, he looked around with a bemused smile. "What's the C.F.T.T?" he asked. "That's a secret, only the members know that," I said in seeming triumph, but in fact melancholy had taken hold of me. The frost had left the ground and a gentle rain was falling.

Standing at a little table in the upstairs hallway, I drafted a programme which went as follows: "1. Opening by the president. 2. The president greets those present and explains the reason for the meeting."

After that I could think of nothing. For a long time, I stood staring into the semi-darkness. Finally, I added: "3. Speech in which the following points are discussed: a. a club on the march; b. no members in name only; c. no one can act weird to the members or the president; d. a department is to be set up for construction and applied science, mostly for mills turned by the wind; the head of it is called the mill-builder: it must be someone who has made a lot of windmills before." I copied it all out neatly and rolled up the paper. Then I went to the bedroom and examined the decorations and the glowing lights. Silence was all around; the voices of children on the street and the barking of a dog intruded only from a distance: it was as though the grey sky had muffled all sound like a layer of matted felt.

At a little past three, Werther arrived with his sister. She was a pale, puffy child with a round, flattened face. She wore a knitted dress of orange wool, which served to underscore her lumpishness. She spoke almost in a whisper and burst into giggles each time. We sat down on the beds.

I had turned off the lighting beforehand, but now I turned it on of a sudden. "Ooh," Martha said; Werther looked around indifferently and without comment.

I stood up, went to the writing table and unfolded my sheet of paper. "I hereby declare the great festive meeting of the C.F.T.T. to be officially opened," I said. I rapped the table a few times with my ruler. "Come in," Martha said and started to giggle. "Isn't Dirk coming?" Werther asked. "I don't believe he is," I said gruffly.

"As president of the C.F.T.T., I would like to welcome those present and the prospective member," I said. "Hi, hello," Werther said. "I will now explain the reason for this meeting," I went on. "It is not our intention only to organize festive afternoons: we will have to hold other meetings too, about serious things. We need to make it a good strong club, a club on the march. We don't need members in name only. If members are only members in name and otherwise act weird towards everyone, we don't need them. The next point I would like to discuss is the fact that there are members who act weird towards other club members or the president. We can't have that. Honoured members! A department will be set up for construction and applied science, mostly for mills run by the wind. The head of it is called the mill-maker: it

44

should be someone who has built lots of mills before. Or someone who is very good at connecting electrical wires for lamps, because that has something to do with it. That's what I have to say," I concluded, crumpled up the piece of paper and sat down beside Werther. "The afternoon meeting has begun," I said vaguely.

Thirty seconds passed during which no one said a thing. "When is it going to start?" Werther asked. "Many of the members have not shown up," I replied. "It's a waste to put on a whole programme for a couple of people." Werther now suggested that we go and fetch Dirk. The three of us went to his house.

Dirk opened the door himself. "Let me have a word with you," I said. "A while ago we were on the dyke and some things happened that weren't very pretty," I started in. "There is no use in trying to find out right here whose fault it was," I went on. "But today the club is having a rollicking festive afternoon, at my house. I'm sure you realize that the deputy-secretary cannot be absent: the entire board needs to be there. It's going to be a lovely afternoon, one which will live on in our memories for a long time. I am also going to give a resounding speech."

After some convincing, he went with us. When we got back to the bedroom, my mother came with tea and sugar cookies. Once we had finished these, a silence fell that seemed to be without end. I stepped to the window and looked at the sky. Then I slipped downstairs to find my brother. "We're all up in the room and we don't have a programme," I said. "Would you come up and play something on your mandolin?" "No," he said. "But we don't have a programme!" I insisted. "No," he repeated, "I'm not doing that." I went on urging him for quite some time, but he stuck by his refusal.

When I got back to the bedroom, I saw that someone had opened the walk-in closet. I had locked it beforehand but left the key in the door. It was the closet I used for two purposes: because it was so dark and quiet, it was where I wielded my member, and also where I moulded pots, canisters and ashtrays from modelling clay, which I left there to dry. A bright, bare bulb illuminated the little space, so that I could close the door all the way behind me (I usually locked it from the inside).

They had all forced entry to it and taken out pots, the better to see them by daylight. "We won't break anything," Werther said. Looking at the bottom of an ashtray, he discovered the inscription C.F.A.T. "What does that mean, C.F.A.T?" he asked. It was an abbreviation for Ceramic Factory of Ancient Times, but I was reluctant to say that.

"They're just letters," I replied. "But they're on everything," he persisted, for he was examining the bottoms of all the other objects now. "That may very well be," I said. "But let's put everything back now."

While they were putting the objects away, Werther dropped one of the pots. It shattered to powdery pieces on the floor. "That's a pity," he said and stood there looking at it. I began pacing back and forth in agitation. When everything was back in place, I locked the closet, stuck the key in my pocket and sat down on the bed. Once again, a silence filled the room.

"Now we're going outside," I said, turning off the lamps. We stumped down the stairs without speaking a word and made our way to the back door. "I have to do my homework now," I said flatly. They remained in the doorway. "You have to leave," I said. "I'm staying here. You people have nasty habits."

Dirk went to his house, but Werther and his sister remained where they were. Without another word, I punched him hard a few times, causing him to cry out, then jumped back inside and slammed the door loudly.

For a long time, I stood at the window of the empty bedroom. A few pine needles rained down from the boughs. "The silence sails like a ship," I thought.

The next day it rained. After school that afternoon I found a letter in our mailbox, which turned out to be from Werther. It read: "Elmer. I don't want you to come to my house any more. You punch people, because

47

you're mean. The club is finished, because I don't want to any more. Werther." It was written in pencil on half a sheet of notebook paper.

I called Dirk to come outside right away and showed him the paper, but moved it and held it at a distance so that he could not quite read it. "This is a secret thing, it just arrived," I said. "It's a letter. We need to have a meeting right away."

We went to the shed. There I let him read the letter. "As a good member of the club, you of course realize what is going on," I said. "He is a really bad spy. He snuck into the club to tell the enemy everything: that's how he wants to destroy the club. He's been working on it for a while. He opened the president's closet so he could smash nice things. That was to ruin the club. We need to bury the list of members in a secret place."

Dirk went on squinting at the letter but said nothing. As he read he picked nonchalantly at a scab on his knee.

"Did you know that a club with only two members is a really good thing?" I asked. "It's actually much better than three." Dirk dropped the letter and groped around on the ground until he found an empty syrup tin. He tried to pry off the lid with his nails. Suddenly I began to hate him.

"You have to get out of the club too," I said. "You've been turned against it, I can tell right away. You want the club to stop too. From now on, you're banned." Dirk said nothing, simply went on picking at the tin. I stood up.

"You have to leave the meeting," I said. "If you want to get back into the club (but that is very hard), you'll have to send a letter to the president and ask forgiveness. Are you going to do that?"

I gave him no chance to reply but started kicking him sullenly. "You ruin everything," I said. When he did not stand up, I grabbed his arms and pulled him upright, then pushed him outside. I watched as he sauntered off without a word.

It was no longer raining but the air was moist; the wind had died down completely and banks of mist rolled slowly across the rooftops. I went back to the shed. On a piece of cardboard I wrote: "There are enemies of the club everywhere." I folded it up tightly and buried it in a shallow hole in the ground, which I marked with a branch from the elderberry bush.

In the days that followed I spoke to neither Dirk nor Werther. The cold snap continued; I stopped going to the shed and spent much more time in the attic. There

I sat alone for long periods. I called the attic space "The Enchanted Castle", and to the door I nailed a cardboard sign with those words written on it in coloured pencil.

On a Wednesday afternoon, when there was no school, I opened an attic window to let in a little grey cat that had been sitting on the roof, coughing in the rain. I locked the animal in the drawer of a big cabin trunk and left it in there for hours. When I opened it again, the bottom of the drawer, which was lined with wallpaper, was messed with a viscous slime. I tossed the animal back onto the roof, across which it limped off, racked with coughs. "It coughed, that's why it had to be teased," I said aloud, looking out through one of the panes at the cat as it moved away. It was the spot where I often stood, thinking and looking outside.

When I could think of nothing to do I spent my time crumbling the soft plaster from the attic walls, which I knocked off with a hatchet. Afterwards I always felt sad, and tried, if I had my glass cutter with me, to scratch my name in a windowpane, almost never with success; then I would go outside again.

On the street behind ours, in a house with a garden adjoining our own, a boy by the name of Maarten Scheepmaker had moved in. One afternoon shortly after he arrived, I happened to be building a fire in the garden. He approached and asked if I was allowed to do that. That was how we met. I was invited to visit his home.

He was my age, but smaller and stockier. He dressed very sloppily, and his lank, greasy hair was always in need of cutting. A wispy moustache already graced his upper lip. He was beset by a penetrating body odour, which I ascribed to the fact that he wore the same warm clothes indoors and out, and that he kept his scarf wrapped around his neck inside the house as well. I enjoyed visiting him, for his habits were singular and strange.

Suspended from thin wires at shoulder height in his little bedroom on the street side were the bones of skeletons, and beneath a bell jar, on a dot of white cotton wool, lay the broken-off, porcelain breasts of a pink female figurine; the shattered remains of the figurine were kept in a box beside them. Around and above his bed, which stood in the middle of the room, he had fashioned a canopy of cloths and rugs, and the walls were filled with panoramas cut from magazines and picture postcards showing sunsets over mountain landscapes.

Except for the bed and one chair, there was no other furniture in the room; the rest of the space was occupied with odds and ends that one had to step over; Maarten was a tinkerer and a builder.

I considered him an inventor. One afternoon, shortly after we met, he told me that one could catch a lot of fish in the ring canal around the city by producing an explosion under water. While I was there he put together a complicated apparatus, consisting of an old cocoa tin with two nails in it which he had magnetized; suspended between the tips of the nails was a string of iron filings. To both nails electrical wires were attached, insulated in such a way as to admit neither water nor air. Beforehand, at the bottom of the tin, he had added a thick layer of a mixture of potassium chlorate and sugar.

"That is one of the worst exploders," he said.

His intention, once the contraption had been placed under water, was to send an electrical charge into it that would cause the string of filings to glow and so ignite the charge. We had just finished our preparations when his mother walked into the room.

She was a short, ugly woman with a weary face and drab, lifeless hair. At first I had considered her a menace, but she was kind-hearted. She had overheard our plan and expressed her concern about it. "What am I going to tell Elmer's parents if the two of you are picked up?" she asked. "Don't you know that they've shot and killed plenty of people for less?" She forbade us to carry out the plan and left the room.

Her words were a mystery, but as I repeated them to myself I felt a bleakness pressing down upon me. I no longer felt like carrying out the plan. "We'd be better off doing something else," I said. "In fact, there's a club that needs to be set up: perhaps you know that too. It's very important. Then we'll just stay here and set it up right away."

I spoke these last words quietly, but in a rush, keeping a careful eye on Maarten the whole time. "The president needs to be someone who has set up clubs before," I said, "then he will appoint a maker right away. That needs to be someone who is good at building things. The maker will build all kinds of things for the board and the president, which they are allowed to keep. He also has to make a lamp that can't be turned off." (That such a thing existed seemed possible to me.)

Maarten appeared not to listen. "Maybe you don't like clubs," I said sagely, "but I once felt the very same way." Maarten inspected the cocoa tin without speaking a word. He announced that he wanted to go ahead with the explosion.

As evening fell, we carried the accoutrements to the waterfront. Maarten switched on the current, but nothing happened. When we pulled the apparatus out of the water, only the electrical wires came up: the tin and all its parts were gone. I expressed my disappointment and my conclusion that the assembly had been faulty, so that everything came loose even before the current was turned on. Maarten assured me passionately, however, that the explosion had actually taken place, but at a great depth, causing the gases to condense and evaporate before they could reach the surface. He spat as he spoke and wiped saliva from his chin, for he was drooling with excitement.

For a moment I found myself doubting whether the apparatus had not perhaps ignited after all; once again, though, I came to the conclusion that it had not, yet I had no desire to press this. What interested me more was whether Maarten himself believed his own explanation. In point of fact, I could not establish whether or not this was the case, but I understood that either conclusion gave cause for dejection.

We returned home; Maarten asked me to come in, but I bade him farewell. In our attic, I began drafting a text. At the top of the paper I wrote: "The new club, which Maarten has to be in. He must become a member." I remained seated, thinking, but could think of nothing more to write. I folded up the paper and placed it in a shallow cardboard box, which already contained thirteen penny coins; this I hid beneath a roofing tile, beside one of the attic windows.

Another time, on a Saturday afternoon, Maarten suggested that we build a rocket. He had a small wooden aircraft bomb somewhere, painted silver with four tailfins at the back; it had once been a toy of his.

He drilled a cavity in the base of the rocket and hammered a tube into it. This he filled with the same mixture used in our previous experiment; to keep the explosive from falling out, he sealed the tube with a paper disc through which he had poked a cotton thread soaked in methylated spirits by way of a fuse.

"Is it going to take off with a bang, or will it start hissing first?" I asked. "Both," he replied. "It's bound to go up twenty-eight metres or so, maybe even higher."

In the garden, on the strip of pavement before our kitchen door, we built a launching pad from a few bricks. He placed the rocket on this, resting on its tailfins with its nose pointed up, and stuffed a wad of paper underneath it, which he lit with a serious expression; we stepped back cautiously. The flame reached fuse and charge, and the tube began to hiss and spit fire. The rocket fell on its side and went on hissing, then fell silent. A wisp of smoke rose up and was quickly dispersed. "It's empty," I said. Maarten picked it up. On the paving stones before the kitchen door was a burn mark, greyish-blue and white at the edges. "There was just enough charge in it to make it fall over," I said, but

Maarten did not agree. "It got stuck on something," he declared roundly. He claimed and insisted that the bomb, while standing upright and while on its side as well, had become caught on something which had impeded it in its motion. I did not believe that but did not want to say so.

"Let's fill it again and set it off," I said, but he waved aside this suggestion. "I have to take a good look at everything before we do that," he said solemnly. "And besides, it has to cool off first. Or did you think it didn't get hot inside there?"

He had taken absolutely no precautions to keep the experiment a secret; his father, who was standing at the window in their back room, had seen everything. But he did not come outside, or even make the slightest gesture. His father was a fat, ponderous man with heavy jowls and dark bags beneath his eyes; his hair was short and bristly. He looked, I thought, like the old mouse from the book of nursery rhymes I still owned. He stared into the gardens with a vague, dreamy expression. It was late in the afternoon and darkness was falling. I tried, to no avail, to stave off the approaching sadness.

Maarten examined the bomb's underside and picked at it. I felt the desire to make him trip or to destroy some article of his clothing: he would then, I thought, start crying almost soundlessly.

Saying it was time for dinner, I left and went to the attic, where I continued hacking at the wall as quietly as I could. The grit I swept onto a little pile; I began hacking away, with purpose now, and made a hole which I gouged out even further with a piece of iron. Taking the old label from a suitcase, I wrote my name and the date on it, rolled it up and stuffed it into the opening. My final step was to fill the hole with an old newspaper. As I was tearing the paper into strips I came across a death notice and scanned a few lines of it. The final sentence, before the names of the family and friends, read: "He has completed his pilgrimage upon this earth." I found myself thinking about that for a long time. I repeated the words slowly to myself and began singing them quietly out loud. I tore out the notice, chewed it to a pulp and jammed it into the hole in the wall. Then I went looking for the glass cutter, but could not find it. Leaning my forehead against a windowpane and touching my member, I listened keenly to the sounds from the house below. "The day is full of signs," I repeated to myself over and over. I thought about asking Maarten up to the attic.

On a Saturday afternoon not long afterwards, the two of us were sitting in his room. We came up with the plan to bag ducks in the watercourse that ran past the cemetery. It was a place rarely visited in autumn and winter. Maarten, as it turned out, owned an air pistol that could be used to fire darts or lead pellets. Although the pellets easily pierced the cardboard box we had set up as a target, the gun's range was extremely limited. Maarten, though, was convinced that we could use it to bring down birds, other animals and even humans. "Did you think you couldn't kill someone with this?" he asked. "It's not even that hard. It just depends where you hit them."

There were, he claimed, eight spots on the human body that were fatal when struck by a projectile. I asked him what those where, but he gave no answer. "You can shoot something at least a hundred metres away," he said, "and then it still has enough power." We fired at an apple; the darts and pellets did not pass all the way through the fruit but disappeared, causing almost no damage to the skin, into the core, where they were hard to recover. I expressed my reservations about the weapon's firepower.

To gain an impression of the pistol's possibilities, we then proceeded to shoot at each other in accordance with pre-established rules; each stood on one side of the room, so we could aim only under the canopy: this precluded the risk of shooting each other in the face. We used darts. After drawing lots, Maarten was allowed the first shot.

He hit me in the middle of the chest. After penetrating my clothes without damaging them, the dart punched a clean little cavity in my flesh. It hardly bled at all and caused me almost no pain. I was enraged but did not show it.

When my turn came, even after taking long aim, I knew the shot would fail. I hit Maarten on the right side of the chest, but his skin remained untouched.

When I stepped over to examine the results, I saw that the little projectile had been blocked by a wad of papers in his inside pocket. It had, however, gone through almost all the pages. I felt the urge to take these papers away and make him beg me to give them back, for I believed that they contained secrets. Yet I did not touch them.

After dinner that evening, under cover of darkness, we set out. I was allowed to carry the pistol and wore it against my bare skin.

The public gardens, which had no fences around them, lay vacant before us. Because the watercourse had been excavated only a few years earlier, the undergrowth was still low; we were able to see over the clumps of bushes and low trees. It was drizzling.

Stepping off the gravel path, we walked on the grassy verge so that our footsteps were almost inaudible.

Soon we arrived at a spot where dozens of ducks were huddled together on the shore. I cocked the pistol and fired into their midst. Startled by the sound, several of the ducks took a few steps towards the water, but that was all. I loaded a second dart and handed the pistol to Maarten. When he fired, all the birds flew off, quacking loudly. We then searched the area but found no other birds. In the end we wandered around the gardens to see if there was anything else of interest there, but found nothing.

"You can't shoot through a coat of feathers," I said. I declared the enterprise an amusing one, perhaps, but altogether futile. Maarten countered my arguments forcefully. He claimed that my shot had gone wide, but that his had struck a duck in the breast and tossed pin feathers into the air. "You saw that, didn't you?" he asked. "That the feathers were knocked off and floated around?" "I couldn't see anything, not very clearly," I replied blandly, for I knew there was no truth in it.

He went on to say that the wounded animal would not have been able to fly far, but would have landed somewhere and bled to death. The next day, he was sure, we would find it. We walked back without a word.

I went into his house with him. His parents were out. In his room, he did not turn on the electric light but lit a candle. Then he removed the fitting from the ceiling and connected the wires to a contraption that crackled and emitted blue sparks. He had taken it from a wooden box. As soon as it was functioning, he blew out the candle and we watched in silence.

The apparatus was made from two Meccano girders, with carbon rods from an old battery attached to the ends; the tips of the rods had been placed close together and between them hung a blue, crackling flame. The whole thing was mounted on a plank, which Maarten placed on the floor. He invited me to sit beside him on the edge of the bed and watch. We slid the canopy aside.

"It's not even a powerful current," he said. "I used resistors in it. You can touch the rods, no problem, it won't give you a shock." He urged me to try it, but I did not dare. To distract from that fact, I asked whether the contraption never turned itself off; he did not reply. I sniffed up the odour from the sparks and stared into the darkness. Maarten's face was only vaguely visible in a blue sheen.

His parents came home soon afterwards. Maarten hurried to put away the contraption but did not light the candle. Instead, he listened tensely and told me to sit perfectly still. Our breathing was measured and quiet. Stepping into the room, his mother felt around for the light switch and mumbled something; she remained standing there for a moment. I pressed my hands between my thighs and listened to the hissing silence. My heart pounded, for I thought that if we were discovered something horrible would happen.

When she had left again, Maarten still did not turn on a light. We remained sitting in darkness. "We have to keep our voices down," he said. I opened my mouth but said nothing. Staring wide-eyed into the darkness, I squeezed my privates hard, to see how much force I would have to apply before the pain came. I felt an urgent need to escape. "I have to go home," I said nervously, "otherwise I'm in big trouble."

Maarten let me out through the window. I ran home quickly and crept up to the attic. Although the electric light was working, I lit a candle that I kept in the cabin trunk. Then I opened the window, pulled the cardboard box from under the roofing tile and took out a sheet of paper. The window I left open in order to hear the wind, which was rattling a far-off gate (for a strong breeze was blowing now).

"I am in the Enchanted Castle," I wrote in pencil on the back of the paper, "but it is the ark of Death. I know that: it is going to sink into the depths."

A gust of air blew in, causing the candle flame to wobble and casting the shadow of my head to and fro across the white expanse of wall. It looked like a huge black bird, wingless yet by some magic power still able to fly and only waiting to do me harm.

As I folded up the paper I began to have my doubts about the best place to hide it. Stuffing it into the wall alongside the rolled-up label seemed risky, for my brother would probably discover the hole. The spot beneath the roofing tile seemed equally unreliable, for neighbourhood boys might see me from their gardens and betray the hiding place to my brother. I decided to fold it up tightly and keep it in my trouser pocket. The thirteen penny pieces I left in the box, which I returned to its place. I remained sitting by the candle until it was time for me to go to bed,

Just before noon of the next day, Maarten came to fetch me, to look for the duck that had supposedly been wounded. We set out right away. In case we saw fish in the water, I took along a scoop net and a jam jar. The weather was as drizzly as the day before; it seemed as though dusk was already falling by morning.

We combed the area where we had been the evening before but found nothing. I had expected no different and looked around with only partial interest. The grey sky lent the watercourse a tarnished, turbid colour; I believed it was possible that water monsters covered in eelgrass lived at the bottom of it (something I had thought before), and that they could come up and seize us by our manly parts and drag us into the depths. I therefore glanced at the surface with some regularity.

When it was clear that the search would be fruitless, Maarten stated that we had started too late and that others had taken the bird with them. I did not argue with him. We walked on and followed a narrow, shallow ditch that we tested with the scoop net. There was little to see in the water. Nonetheless, I did pull up an elongated, beetle-like creature with little claws. It was about the size of half an index finger. I did not dare to touch it, and so lifted it between two sticks; then I tossed it as far from the water as I could, into the grass. I was uneasy about this, however, and went looking for the animal and stamped it into the ground with my heel. "They're nasty creatures, I've read that," I told Maarten. "It has to be killed." In fact, though, I wanted to make sure the beetle did not make its way back to the water, for then it would surely tell the water monsters about me.

Very soon we came to a spot where the water was low, where attempts had seemingly been made to build a dam: branches and stones clogged the water there and made it shallow. Close by I found a large gramophone horn in the shape of a calyx, almost completely submerged in the ditch. We fished it out. At its widest spot it measured three-quarters of a metre. The outside of the horn was painted green, the inside was a light pink. Here and there the paint had chipped away. "It's mine," I said, "because I'm the one who found it. When you find something, for example, and you're the first to point to it, then it belongs to you."

I rinsed off the horn, shook it dry and bellowed into it. Then I began clowning about. "Hear ye, hear ye," I yelled into the horn, "performing for you now is the huge elephant Jumbo. Hello, you dirty bastards!" Meanwhile, we walked on. I laid the horn over my shoulder, with the opening facing back, so that I could go on hooting into it. "The person who has this horn is awfully powerful," I thought.

"Listen, Maarten," I said. "We've talked about the club before, but now it really has to be set up. We must not wait any longer, because you know very well that people are setting up enemy clubs everywhere." When he did not react to my words, I went on: "If we set up the club this afternoon, we've already got a horn. And a club with a horn is just the thing, I'm sure you know that. We can blow it when the meeting is about to begin. The best thing, of course, is if the president does that. That way everyone can tell that it's a good club."

Maarten barely seemed to hear. With my net he scooped a few little fishes out of the ditch and put them in the jam jar. "If we have a club we can catch fish too and build a pond together," I said, already partly in despair.

At that moment, an unfamiliar boy in blue overalls came walking towards us. He was a good head taller than me and had a pale, bony face and extremely light blond hair. Leering, he walked up to me, stopped, looked at the horn and tapped it with his index finger. I began shaking.

His eyes were small and set deep in his head. Along his upper lip I saw crusty swellings, like a skin condition. He grinned, tapped the horn again, now a bit harder, and asked, without looking at Maarten, where I had found it. I clutched the instrument to my breast and at first could come up with nothing to say.

"We pulled it out of the ditch here," I said at last. "It was in there for a long time already, because some-one threw it away: it wasn't anyone's." I wanted to say more but didn't know what. I looked at Maarten, but he said nothing. "Well as long as you know it's mine," the boy said. "You two don't go taking things away around here that I put down there. You hear me, little boy? Give me that thing, and quick."

"We need it really badly," I said quietly, but I knew the horn was lost. The boy grabbed hold of it, pulled it away from me and sauntered off. We remained stand-ing and watched him go. Then we walked home. The rain, which had until now been almost imperceptibly fine, grew heavier.

"It doesn't matter," I said, "it was a shitty old thing anyway. No good to anyone. That's easy to tell. I have an uncle, by the way, who has a whole bunch of those horns; I can get as many as I like." Maarten did not reply; he held up the jam jar and examined the fish.

"We need to set up the club right away this afternoon," I said. "Then we'll form an army, because every good club has one. The president of the club will be the commander in chief: that's always the way it goes." Maarten shook the jam jar and went on staring at the fish.

When we got to my house, I asked him to come up to the attic. There I opened the little window and showed him the box beneath the roofing tile. "That's the club's secret spot," I said. "Everything that gets written down, we save in there: that's the cave, because no one can get to it."

I found some paper, laid it on top of the cabin trunk and invited Maarten to help me draw up the first document. "First we need an army," I said, "because a club is nothing without an army." I asked him to wait, and quickly wrote down a few things. Then I read it out loud: "1. The club has an army, that can also hunt down people. If there is someone, for example, who steals horns all the time, we go after him. Then he is taken prisoner." I saw that Maarten was looking at the sealed-up hole in the wall. It had stopped raining; bright patches were moving across the sky.

"So now the club has been set up," I continued loudly. "It is called the New Army Club, the N.A.C." This last sentence I wrote down after the number 2. Maarten, I thought, was listening now, but he did not seem enthusiastic.

"You do understand, I trust, that it's very important that we have an army?" I asked. "If the club wants to, we can capture that son of a bitch who stole our horn. Because I know his name and I know where he lives."

"Who is it, then?" Maarten asked. This question placed me in a predicament. "That has to remain a secret," I answered, "because the army isn't entirely ready yet." My precise meaning was unclear to me as well. I quickly folded up the piece of paper, placed it in the cardboard box and slipped it back beneath the roofing tile. "It is completely hidden now," I said. "No need to worry that anyone will find it. If it starts raining, for example, it will stay dry, because the tile's on top of it." I turned and picked up the jam jar that Maarten had placed on the floor and emptied it onto the roofing tile. Maarten cried out, but then calmly joined me in watching as the fish were washed away and disappeared down the drainpipe. "They're going into the ground, because they are absolutely filthy animals," I said to myself. The jam jar itself I tossed into the garden, where it landed without breaking. I closed the window and moved to stand behind the cabin trunk, as though it were a counter. From there I looked at Maarten, who was still peering out of the window. "He is the cat and has to go in the trunk," I thought.

"You don't have to join up today," I said persuasively. "If you're not completely sure, better wait till tomorrow. Because getting into the club right away is easy enough, but then you might become a member in name only."

Maarten started poking at the cavity in the wall and plucking little pieces from the paper that filled it. "That's another thing that we'll put in the club rules," I said. "Club members do not ruin things at each other's house. Anyone who does so gets kicked out." On a second sheet of paper I wrote: "3. When there is a meeting at someone's house, no one is allowed to break anything. Anyone who does so gets kicked out." I read this aloud to Maarten, picked up the hatchet and began knocking at the plaster at a spot a little further from the hole. Suddenly, Maarten announced that it was time for him to go home. As he was going down the stairs I observed him closely, then slipped back quietly into the attic. Removing the sheet of paper from my pocket, I crossed out what was written on both sides and wrote: "PLANT TORTURES. You can nail a twig from a plant to the fence while it is still on the plant. Then it dies slowly. You can also cut it and then rub ink on it, so it gets into the twig, then it gets a completely different colour and it dies, but that takes a long time." Leaving a space between paragraphs, I wrote beneath this: "When there is a mushroom, you can light a fire of matchbooks underneath it. Then it gets roasted from the bottom up, while it is still in the ground, because it is still there." In a final paragraph, I wrote: "If there are spiders on a plant, you have to build a fire under it too. Then it can't get away any more." Realizing that my trousers pockets were not safe enough, I folded the paper and stuck it beneath my shirt, next to the skin.

I called our cat, a grey with white spots, up to the attic and cuddled her for a while. Then I went downstairs and fetched a few biscuits. Returning, I took a long, rectangular crate that had once contained tea and placed it in unsteady balance at the top of the stairs, with the opening towards me. I fed the cat a few pieces of biscuit, then tossed the last bits into the crate. When the animal climbed in, its weight threw the whole thing out of balance and it crashed, crate and all, down the stairs. I observed the fall closely. Then I went back to reread the text about plants. Just as I was about to fold it up again, I heard my brother coming up the stairs; I stuffed the piece of paper into my mouth and ate it.

Monday morning was rainy as well; the afternoon remained overcast. After coming home from school, I was about to go to the attic when I discovered that my mother was hanging up laundry there. Despite the chill in the air, I went to sit in the storage shed. When I started feeling too cold, I lit some methylated spirits in a tin and stared into the faint, motionless glow. "This is the religious flame," I said solemnly. I caught a harvest spider and tossed it into the fire. "Sacrifices are brought in from all sides," I said, half singing the words. From time to time I got up and looked into Maarten's garden.

When I saw him at last, I extinguished the spirits and sauntered over with seeming indifference. He was wearing his raincoat and looking up at the sky. "Is it going to rain?" he asked. "I think so," I said, "but not hard." Hastily, I added: "It doesn't matter if the weather's bad, because I already have a clubhouse where we can hold a meeting; it's always there for us to use." Maarten went on looking at the sky. "It's over there," I said, pointing at the storage shed. "There may be members who think it's not so good, because it's cold, but we're allowed to have a fire. That's a flame in a pot. It's on the ground in front of the president and it doesn't go out and you don't have to throw any wood onto it." I asked him to come along and see, but he told me he had to run an errand to a clockmaker's, to pick up something that had been repaired. I went with him.

For a long time, we walked without a word. At last I broke the silence. "You can still join the club," I said. "Or don't you like the name, the New Army Club?" I brought it to his attention that a new meeting could be held. When he replied that he saw no sense in a club with two members who also happened to live almost next door to each other, I suggested that we recruit new ones. "But I don't even want to join a club," Maarten said at last. We were silent again for a long while. Once more, I was the first to speak. "Are you the kind of person who gets scared awfully fast?" I asked. "Not at all," he replied. "Still, I figured you weren't particularly brave," I persisted. "You actually don't look very brave. I don't believe you have a lot of gumption." He said nothing back. All the way to the clockmaker's, we did not exchange a word.

The shop was down a narrow street. We paused in front of it, for there was something in the display window that called for our attention. It was a composite machine, which I first took to be a set of scales. Upon closer examination, however, it turned out to be a machine with no other purpose than to amuse and astound the general public.

At the top of it, metal bearings of various sizes dropped regularly into a copper basin, upon which a large pointer showed their weight. Then the balls fell further into the buckets of a paddle wheel, which was driven by them. The power from this wheel was transmitted obliquely to a very long arm, which protruded from the machine and moved up and down a few centimetres each time. The arm bore two tracks, parallel to each other and separated by miniature hoarding, for a model racing car that drove up the one side and down the other without stopping: cleverly constructed connecting curves at the ends allowed the little car to make the turn and drive on without crashing or rolling over. I found the vehicle quite moving. It was a little red car with white plates saying W 13. In light-blue lettering on the black flag that the driver held in his hand were the words: "The Death Drive". His head and face were covered by a crash helmet and a leather mask. In front of the apparatus was a sign in block letters, with the text: "This *perpetuum mobile*, Racing Car Track, was constructed from 871 pieces over a period of fourteen months (all parts are handmade) by a disabled mine worker, who is trying to support himself in this way. The postcards are available for twenty cents apiece or from J. Schoonderman, 8 Beukenplein, ground floor. One guilder and seventy-five cents for ten."

All around the machine lay faded postcards bearing a picture of the apparatus. They were covered in a thick layer of dust. "It's a fine thing," I said. In actual fact, I felt a great sadness drawing near. "I have to go and see someone," I said nervously, when Maarten made to enter the shop. "I forgot about that: I don't have any time." Before he could reply, I had taken off at a trot and was down the street. When I was sure that he would not catch up with me, I stopped by the ditch at the side of the road and looked about for pieces of wood, but saw nothing floating there. Ducking into a doorway, I waited for Maarten to pass. Once he had gone by, I stepped out and followed him all the way home at a distance. "I am walking behind him, but he doesn't know that I am following him," I said to myself.

Nearing my own home, I peered around carefully and caught sight of Maarten in his garden. I could not go up to the attic yet, and so I decided to walk on for a bit. The weather was not particularly cold; the fine rain felt lukewarm. I walked past Werther's house and turned off into the parklands along the dyke. There, after looking around a bit, I waded into the bushes.

The ground, which was sodden and sucked at my shoes, was covered in moss here and there. I found a spot from which I could observe Werther's house without being seen by passers-by. There I settled down on

74

a broken trunk, which hurt me when I sat on it, and pondered. As it turned out, I had a pencil stub in my pocket, but no paper. On the ground, however, I found a wet cigar box. On it I wrote: "I am sitting in the spy tower watching Werther's house. At the moment I don't see anything. If I see trouble I will send a messenger." I threw down the box, stomped on it and drove it into the ground with my heel.

Just as I was doing this, I heard the approaching sound of cheers and laughter. A woman hurried by on the broad gravel path; every once in a while she slowed and turned on her heels. At first I thought she was doing this in order to look behind her, but in fact it seemed more like a set of dance steps. Before I could entirely verify my observation, she had passed from sight. I stepped out of the bushes to watch her go; just as I reached the path I was met by a group of no fewer than thirty shouting children, who seemed to be pursuing her. I blended in with them and was swept along. We gained ground on the woman. When she reached the street, she stepped off the kerb and waited. Her pursuers came to a halt at a little distance. I was at the back of the group.

The woman turned and curtsied, seizing the hems of her skirts on both sides. When she straightened up, I saw that it was Werther's mother. A deep fear took hold of me. Afraid that she would pick me out in the crowd, I bent my knees and squatted a little. "She's not wearing a coat," I thought.

She began performing a series of rapid steps in place, clacking the soles of her shoes loudly on the paving stones each time. Suddenly she lifted her skirts up above her head, almost throwing herself off balance. When she had let them fall again, she paused for a moment and then resumed dancing, with smaller, more cautious steps this time, humming a tune loudly as she did.

At that moment two women came out of a nearby doorway, one of them wearing a white cap, like a nurse's. The other had a coat tossed over her shoulder. They took Werther's mother carefully by the arms. "Mrs Nieland, you need to come inside quickly," the woman with the cap said. "It's much too cold out here. It's already late. You need to come home right now."

They kept their grip on her. Although she seemed to struggle, she did not resist with any real force. We moved closer.

"I'm dancing to the music," Werther's mother said. "I am Agatha, the dancer." She said this in a normal, businesslike tone, but then went on testily: "Everyone shouldn't act as though he knows what dancing is. Dancing is something very different from what people think it is." The two women pulled her along, gently but firmly. Her dark floral dress ballooned now and then in the wind, which lifted her wispy hair. I felt like running away but could not make myself.

Suddenly, she began shouting. "Education!" she bellowed. "This isn't what you call education! It's not even close!" Her face was fatigued and flushed, but she went on smiling. The two women pulled her along more quickly now and herded her through the door of her own house.

A few adults had joined us in the meantime, including the corner tobacconist. He watched but said nothing.

Although it was no longer necessary, I went on squatting at the back of the crowd. A little girl pushed me, and I fell over. "I bet you're taking a big poop," she said. Werther's front door had closed. I took a few feinting steps in one direction, then turned and ran all the way home. I realized that I would have to think deeply about this.

In the garden, after dinner, I lit a wood fire in an old iron barrel and remained standing beside it. The sides of the barrel grew red-hot. I called to Maarten to come and have a look. We passed water against the iron, which threw up clouds of steam. When the fire had died down, he suggested that we take a large cardboard box that was in his garden, fill it with flammable material and float it on the water. We put together

77

everything we needed and went to the watercourse. After steadying the box, which was filled with wood shavings, pieces of cardboard and dry branches and had a paving stone at the bottom by way of ballast, we lit it and shoved it away on the water. The wind was unfavourable, though, and blew it back slowly in our direction. We gave it another shove, but this time too it returned slowly to shore. Maarten said that if he'd had the air pistol with him, he could have sunk the box with only a shot or two. The cardboard vessel burned slowly down to just above the waterline, became sodden and went out with a hiss, after which it sank. We sat down on the bank.

The light had left the sky, but above the cemetery grounds we could see smoke rising and billowing in our direction. It smelled of smouldering, incomplete combustion. "That's where they burn the bones," Maarten said. "When the dead people have been in the ground for seven years, all the flesh is off them." To this he added even more details. The bones hanging in his room, he said, he had taken from huge charnel heaps in the graveyard, in winter when the ditches were frozen. He had done this in collaboration with others. They had also taken skulls, but lost them again, because during their retreat across the ice they had played football with them, not knowing that the graveyard personnel were in pursuit. They escaped at the last moment but had to leave the skulls behind. By the time they came back, the thaw had set in and the ice had already cracked open.

I did not know whether it was true. Finally, though, he claimed that there had still been hair on some of the skulls. This was a detail I thought impossible to invent, and so now I believed the whole story. "The day bears three signs," I said to myself: I believed that the dancing of Werther's mother, the continuous return of the burning box and Maarten's story about skeletons were connected in a mysterious way.

When we arrived home, I took Maarten up to the attic and turned on the electric light. Before we were finished climbing the stairs, however, I was already longing to be alone. He looked around inquisitively and examined the cabin trunk. "That's the secret chest," I said. "Don't touch it." I went and stood behind it and took out some paper and a pencil. "As chance would have it, I need to write down something about the club," I said, peering at the paper as though something were already written on it. "The envoy has delivered an urgent message. I need to arrange that, but no non-members may be present." I looked at him pensively. "You have to leave," I ruled, "there is nothing to be done about it." Maarten left without a word. As he was going down the steps, I said: "You're not allowed to come here any more, because there's no way I can associate with enemies of the club."

I lit a candle, turned off the electric light and wrote: "The Army Club. What the Club can do. We can make boxes sail that are burning. That is good for plaguing water monsters. 2. Go into the graveyard when it is freezing and take away bones and skulls. If it is not freezing, we build a dam. That must be done by members who know a lot about digging and building. At the head is a commander in chief, that is the president of the club. 3. Go into the woods and watch, for example, when someone comes by who is running and dancing. You can see that, because she isn't wearing a coat." This last point caused me to think deeply. Beneath what I had written I put the date, hid it beneath the roofing tile and took out a new sheet of paper. I decided to send Werther a letter and wrote: "Werther, I need to talk to you badly, because it is very important. There is danger. I will wait for you tomorrow at four o'clock. On the corner close to your house. Elmer."

I was given permission to go outside for a while. When I reached Werther's and was standing in the doorway, there wafted my way the same odour that I had discerned inside his house. I pushed open the letter box, but rather than tossing in the letter, I put my ear to it and listened, keeping one eye on the street. A draught of air rushed past my ear but that was all, I heard nothing. Still, I stood there listening. After a while I heard the rumble of footsteps in one of the rooms, and muffled voices. I thought about opening the door and then sitting at the bottom of the stairs, but I did not dare.

Suddenly, I heard a door open onto the upstairs landing and recognized the voice of Werther's mother. "I have a lot more power than you people think," she said loudly. "I have the green gemstones that…" (here a few words were lost). Then the door closed again with a fairly loud bang; I could still hear voices, but too faintly to make out the words. At last I tossed the letter through the slot and went home.

On the afternoon of the next day I stood at the appointed place and waited. I had hurried there from school and was confident that Werther's path would soon cross mine, for he attended a private school some twenty minutes' walk away. When I saw him coming, I ran to meet him and walked up with him, launching into a long explanation as I did. "There has been a very bad misunderstanding," I said. "That has to be set aright. We're not enemies at all, but there was someone who wanted to destroy the club: he sowed discord." (This latter expression I had read somewhere that same afternoon.)

Werther was no longer angry and listened willingly. "We have to meet tomorrow afternoon," I said. We had arrived at his front steps. Here he stopped hesitantly. "We have to talk," I said, "that is necessary." Suddenly his mother stuck her head out of a little window that could not have corresponded with a room, or even with the stairwell for that matter. From there she began talking.

"Hello, boys," she shouted, laughing. I wasn't sure whether her comportment was normal or highly peculiar. "Mother, you look just like an acrobat," Werther said. He grinned for a moment, but then looked up again with a straight face.

His mother shook her head comically a few times, then stuck out her chin and asked: "Isn't that your little friend, Elmer? Have the two of you been hatching a plan again? You're such cute little scamps. Come on upstairs."

Werther seemed to waver, but when his mother repeated her request we climbed the stairs. She was waiting for us on the landing. Looking around carefully, I tried to figure out where the window could have been, and concluded that it must have belonged to the water closet.

"I was looking down at the two of you for a long time," she said, "but I didn't say anything. I actually felt like tossing water on your heads. Would you have enjoyed that, Elmer?" she asked.

"It would have been funny," I said, staring at the floor; "although it's still a bit cold out." I felt ill at ease.

We had moved to the kitchen by then. "Cold water helps against dreams," his mother said. "Werther, tell your friend what you dream about all the time."

Leaning on the window sill with one hand, she moved her feet rapidly in a sort of prancing motion. "Go on, tell him," she urged. "He's an odd little fellow, isn't he?" she said, grabbing Werther by the hair. "Are you odd too?" Right away she grabbed my hair as well and gave my head a gentle shake. I did not dare to make the slightest move.

"Well," Werther said, "there's this fellow who chases me all the time. He has a big breadknife and he wants to use it to cut my lips in two." He illustrated this with his index finger, drawing it across his lips in the same gesture with which one calls on others to be silent.

"But we've been to the doctor, Werther," said his mother. "Yes, Elmer," she said, turning to me, "we took little Werther to the doctor. He is oversensitive. He has to be bathed in cold water every afternoon or evening. I'll go run the bath right now. He has to be completely undressed first, of course."

At that moment, Werther's sister came home from school. "You two can go in the bath together," his mother said, "then I'll make the water a little less cold."

Dragging in a large basin from the balcony, she began filling it with a red rubber hose and told Werther and Martha to undress.

"You can take a bath too, if you like," she said to me. "No, that won't be necessary," I said. "I already had one this morning." (There was no truth in this.) "Oh, but it's no problem if you want to take another one here, you know," she said. "Then the three of you can horse around a bit afterwards, until you're nice and dry. There's no reason why you have to get dressed again right away."

She spoke with seeming indifference, but there was in fact something imperious in her voice that frightened me. Werther and Martha had begun to undress. Their clothes they draped over the chair in the kitchen. It struck me that Werther undressed very slowly and looked around bashfully the whole time. His mother told him to hurry up.

"You never have to be ashamed of anything on your body," she said. "It's something very normal. Elmer's going to take a bath with the two of you, isn't he?" "No, not now," I said, "there's no need." "If you don't want to, you don't have to," she went on, "but it is awfully good for you. You sometimes have nasty dreams too, don't you?"

"I dreamed about a whale," I said. I immediately regretted having made this admission and realized that

I should simply have responded in the negative. "But it wasn't nasty at all, it was nice," I added quickly. I thought about turning and running out of the house, but did not, for I might have slipped on the stairs. Martha, who was already naked, said she was cold and raced into the living room.

Werther's mother decided that they did not have to get into the bath immediately: first they would be allowed to walk around undressed.

"You two go inside there and have a wrestling match," she said. "Then I'll come and see who wins." Werther, however, was reluctant to remove his underpants.

"There is really no need for you to hide your little thingamabob," she said. "Your friend has one too. Or don't you?" I nodded feebly and searched for something to say but could not utter a word. I tried to shuffle over to one corner of the kitchen, unseen. Suddenly, though, she approached me from behind, threw an arm around my throat and felt around with the other hand, over my shoulder and down: her breath blew down the back of my neck. I stood stock-still; at the slightest sign of resistance, I knew, she would shove a thin knife or a long needle into my neck until it struck the marrow. It took only a few seconds for her to reach the objective of her groping. Then she let go of me and jumped over to the window. Her face was red. Werther looked into the water in the bath. For the space of a moment, all was silent. "That thingamabob of yours, you two, has a purpose," she said then. "It's there to do something with, something that's not weird at all. Birds do it too."

The front door opened and someone came up the stairs. It was Werther's father. He looked into the kitchen but said nothing. Then we saw him go into the living room, but he left that room again quickly to climb another set of stairs. Coming back down almost immediately, he entered the kitchen and stood there silently. I thought about shaking his hand but did not dare.

The man remained standing silently, as though faced with the need to shed light on matters of some complexity. "Mother," he said then, without looking at anyone, "tomorrow Aunt Truus is coming to take Martha and Werther to a little circus." He spoke this sentence waveringly and looked out of the window to the balcony all the while. Werther's mother said nothing and seemed not to listen. "Agatha," he said. Now she suddenly looked up. "Who did you say is coming to pick up Werther and Martha?" she asked. "What is that all about? What's the good of it?"

Werther, completely naked now, was standing at the door to the balcony. I thought about what it would be like if he were to go outside and jump. "He'd be a dead bird," I thought, looking at him. He looked cold.

"Agatha," Werther's father said, "I'm telling you this so that you'll remember. When Truus gets here, they have to be ready. So they can go with her right away."

"She's taking them to the circus?" his mother asked. "Then I'll go along too, no reason why I can't." "Agatha," Werther's father spoke immediately, "we were going to stay at home tomorrow afternoon, remember? We were going to talk about a few things, that's what we agreed on, didn't we? You know that very well." "Oh," she said, "yes. Tomorrow afternoon we're at home. Nice and cosy. But if the circus is awfully fun, I may go along anyway: just for a few minutes." She smiled and began speaking more quietly, until her voice trailed off imperceptibly at last.

"Werther," the man said, "listen to me. I'm telling you this in case your mother forgets. After lunch I want you two to stay at home and not go outside and don't get dirty." "Yes," Werther said, staring at his father. He went on: "Then Aunt Truus will come and get you and you'll go to a sort of little circus. Will you two remember that?"

"Werther was going to come to my house tomorrow," I said suddenly. "I was going to come by and pick him up and he was going to go along with me." For a moment, I wasn't sure whether I had actually spoken these sentences.

"Well, then, you can go along too," Werther's father said quickly. "Werther, he can go with you." Werther's mother stood wobbling on her feet and staring at the kitchen mat with a rigid smile.

"What is it, where are we going, Father?" Werther asked now.

"It's a sort of variety show," his father replied, "like a circus but smaller. With little animals. There's a man with a dog that jumps through a hoop. You two can have dinner with Aunt Truus. Agatha, Truus has invited them over for dinner."

Werther's mother, who seemed not to be listening, began giggling quietly. Suddenly, addressing no one in particular, she said: "Is that what you call an education? That's no education. That has nothing to do with anything." She had stopped moving her feet.

"Werther, go and get dressed," his father said, "and go into the other room. Take your clothes along to the heater." Werther disappeared. I wished I could follow him, but didn't dare. The three of us remained in the kitchen now. Werther's mother started humming.

"Isn't it time for you to go home, my boy?" his father asked. "Yes, actually, it is," I said, grinning to hide my discomfort. With one hand at the back of my head, he ushered me out of the kitchen and closed the door behind us. Without applying force, yet resolutely, he bustled me along. We came to the landing. "Go quickly now," he said, "otherwise you'll be late." He did not look at me. On the first step down, I stopped. "Sir," I asked, "what time should I be here tomorrow afternoon? I'm allowed to go with them, aren't I?" I considered it possible that he would send me flying down the stairs with a kick, perhaps to the head. He hesitated for a moment, then said that I could come at two o'clock. "What's your name?" he asked. I told him my name was Elmer, said goodbye and hurried down, fearful that he would go looking for the brochure.

At home I told them about the invitation. "Werther's aunt is taking us to a little circus," I said. "What kind of circus?" my mother asked. "It's a kind of miniature circus," I said, "sort of a variety show, with lots of little animals. Monkeys and rabbits. And they've got dogs that go through a hoop." "You didn't go asking that aunt whether you could go along, I hope?" she asked anxiously. "No, absolutely not," I said. "That aunt wasn't even there. It was their own idea for me to go along."

The next afternoon she gave me thirty-five cents, wrapped in a piece of paper. "I want you to give this to that aunt," she said. "You don't have to let other people pay your way for you." Through the paper, I could feel that it was a quarter and a ten-cent piece.

When I rang Werther's bell at ten minutes to two, his father came to the door. "I'm Elmer," I said, "I'm going with them this afternoon." "Would you mind waiting down here?" he asked.

It took a very long time, so long that at times I thought they must already have left. "How can his father be at home during the day?" I wondered. At last, Werther and his sister came out of the house. They were accompanied by a woman who looked a bit like Werther's mother, but younger. She had the same tiny eyes, but her mouth was normal and she wore her hair in a bun. I wanted to shake her hand, but there was no time for that.

"We're running late, kids," she said, "hurry up now." The wind was blowing hard and it was raining. On our way to the bus stop we walked straight into the wind, so no one spoke a word. Once aboard the bus, the aunt said to me: "So you're the friend, Elmer, are you? Nice you could come along." I already had my hand held out to give her the money, but just then the bus pulled away. During the drive, we spoke no more. Werther's aunt regularly handed out peppermints.

At the terminus we got out and walked to the tram. The rain had stopped. It was quiet beneath the glass roof of the tram stop. Werther and his sister sat on the narrow bench, on either side of their aunt. I stayed close by, pacing up and down. They spoke among themselves softly. "That's right," Werther's aunt said, "I'm coming to live with you for a while. Does that sound nice?" I listened.

"Mother is nervous," she went on. "Maybe you two have noticed that already. That's what happens when someone gets very tired. I'm coming to your house to help out a bit."

"There's no need at all for the two of you be sad or frightened when Mother says something you don't completely understand," she went on. "That's because she's tired, and then your thoughts get all mixed up. You know what I mean: you ask something and what she says back is something very different from what you meant." "Yes," Werther said in a half-whisper. His eyes shifted restlessly back and forth. The tram arrived just as I was getting ready to hand over the money, so I could not follow through.

Our destination turned out to be a low building that looked somewhat like a café; it bore, in neon letters, the name "Arena". I could not imagine there being a circus here, because no admission was charged at the door. I thought about drawing this fact to the attention of Werther's aunt, but she led us through the revolving doors with such confidence that I could only assume she knew the way.

The room we entered was low and spacious; the chairs, however, were not arranged in rows, as at a theatre or cinema, but grouped around little tables. There were thirty or forty people inside, eating and drinking and looking at a stage that had been set up in the middle of the room. On that stage was a man of alarming countenance. His head seemed too large for his body, his hair stood straight up and he was peering cross-eyed at the tip of his nose. The toes of his shoes were turned inwards, pointing at one another. Bright-coloured beams of light were fixed on him. He was silent and seemed to be waiting. The people giggled. Just as we were settling down at a table an orchestra began to play and the man sang at an awkward holler: "I'm the knucklehead, I'm the chump, I'm Jopie with the IQ of a bump." Then he cupped his mouth in his hands as though he were vomiting.

It was, as it turned out, the final line of a song, for the curtain fell and people clapped. Of the four of us, Martha was the only one who laughed.

I squinted at the price list on the table. The cheapest thing on it was lemonade, which cost fifty-five cents. This startled me and I tried to put the list back where it had been, but Werther's aunt had seen me reading and asked if there was anything I wanted. "No, not at all," I said quickly. Meanwhile, the curtains had gone up for a new number. It seemed to be a sort of play; I did not understand what it was about. It began thusly: in a room with a folding screen and a desk, two men in white coats were waiting. From the pockets of their coats hung thin rubber tubes. "Doctors have a tough time of it," said one. "You never get a good-looking dish in for an appointment," said the other.

Werther's aunt flagged down the waiter and asked him for a programme, but there was none. "It just keeps on and on and you keep getting something different," he replied. Werther's aunt ordered a cup of coffee for herself and lemonade for the three of us.

The play went on. A fat lady came in with a girl, probably her daughter. She asked for an examination and went behind the changing screen to undress. A few times she came out from behind the screen and glanced left and right. Each time she had taken off more of her clothes, which she hung over the folding screen from the inside. Every time she appeared, the people laughed loudly. The girl, her fingers in her mouth, stood staring at the floor. "Have you ever played doctor?" one of the men asked her. "How do you do that?" asked the girl in a stupid, whiny tone. The people at the tables laughed.

Feeling apprehensive, I decided to stop watching. The lemonade made my nose tingle unpleasantly, and

93

I could make myself sip at it only with great effort. Werther's aunt must have noticed. "You don't have to drink it if you don't want to," she said. Now I pulled the money out of my pocket and devised the plan of tossing the coins, still wrapped in their paper, into her purse.

I kept an eye on Martha and Werther. Martha seemed to find everything that happened on the stage colourful and funny, and laughed throughout. Werther, however, sat staring glumly into space.

Using the rubber hoses, which I recognized now as a stethoscope, one of the doctors set about examining the lady. All the while he went on loudly muttering comments, which met with laughter here and there, but we were sitting too far away to make them out.

My hope had been to toss the wrapped coins with the most fluid of motions into Werther's aunt's open purse, but I missed and the money hit the floor. She heard it and picked it up. "Did this fall off the table?" she asked me. "I don't know," I replied. "Someone must have left it here," she decided, after removing the paper. To my horror, it turned out there was something written on it. She read it out loud: "Milkman, a litre and a half, pay tomorrow." There was nothing else on it, which put my mind slightly more at ease. She felt there was no sense in trying to locate the owner. "You children can use it later to buy some sweets," she said.

Having finished his examination, the doctor declared that the fat lady was in good health. Then he examined the daughter, without her having undressed first. "This one's in bad need of an injection," he said. "Mercy, can you tell that right away?" the mother cried. "She hasn't even taken off her clothes yet." "No," said the other doctor, "we can tell by just looking at her." Then mother and daughter made ready to leave.

"I want your daughter to come in tomorrow afternoon for an appointment, on her own," said the first doctor. "Will it be expensive?" the mother asked. "No, oh no," the doctor assured her, "she'll get the injection for free." "Can it do any harm?" the mother asked then. "No, absolutely not," the doctor assured her. "Sometimes it makes them fat for a while," the other doctor chimed in, "but that goes away by itself."

The audience whooped with merriment. Werther's aunt called the waiter over. "Will the animals be coming on later?" she asked. "The dog with the hoop?" "No, ma'am," the man replied, "that was last week." "And what is on this afternoon?" she persisted. She was told that the programme consisted of sketches, tap dancing and acrobatics. Werther followed their conversation tensely. Suddenly I had the feeling that he perhaps had the same thoughts I did, and that we, without anyone else knowing (for it was being kept a secret), were perhaps brothers.

"This is not really very suitable," his aunt said. "We should be going."

I applied all my willpower to finishing the lemonade. On the stage, the finale began: after having exited to applause, the woman and her daughter returned and drumbeats rolled up from the orchestra. Suddenly all four actors donned wigs that looked as though they were made from absorbent cotton or cotton wool and stepped to the edge of the stage. Then the four of them began swinging their hips to the beat, front and back, and singing in harmony: "Bonking, bonking, bonking, bonking to beat the band, and if they take away our bonking machine, we'll do it again by hand." When it was over they took a bow while the drums rolled anew. We went outside.

"Last week it was quite nice," Aunt Truus said, "but this was not very suitable." I wondered where we were off to. "Why don't the two of you go and buy something," she said suddenly. She handed the coins to Werther and sent the two of us into a grocer's. There were quite a few people queuing there. "Werther," I said as we were waiting, "on Sunday I'd like you to go along to my uncle and aunt's. I got to go with you today, so Sunday you can go with me. You've earned it." We bought dates and peppermint sticks and spent the entire sum. I was about to ask him again to accompany me on Sunday, but we were already out of the shop and standing beside his aunt. She viewed our purchases with approval. It started drizzling. Werther divided up the dates, but they did not appeal to me. "I think I'll be going home," I said. His aunt tried to convince me to stay with them, but I was adamant. "I have to get back early," I said. At last she gave in and asked if I had money for the tram. "Oh yes," I said, although I had none. When she said she would walk with me to the stop, I told her that I wanted to look in a few shop windows along the way and would make it to the tram on my own. I took leave of them with a quick wave. When they were already some distance away, I walked back and asked Werther if I could count on him on Sunday. Before he could reply, I ran off again, but in that brief interval his aunt handed me a peppermint stick, which I accepted. I started on the extremely long walk home and ate it without enjoyment.

"Did you give the money to that boy's aunt?" my mother asked. "Yes, she's got it," I said. "Was it nice?" she asked. "Yes, it was quite amusing," I said flatly, and went to the attic. There I wrote a letter to Werther, which contained the following: "Werther. You should go along on Sunday afternoon, because it is quite amusing. Come to my house as early as you can. When you get home, this letter will already be there." When I left the house to deliver it, it was raining just as it had been when we left for the variety show. In front of Werther's house a white car was parked, with people standing beside it and talking. I walked past them, climbed the outside steps and slipped the letter through the slot. Just as I was doing so, I heard a pounding on the stairs and a clamour of voices, ending in shouts. "Now hold on like that," a high male voice said, "and don't let go." I listened at the letter box and heard thumping, half-stumbling sounds, as though a struggle was going on. At that moment a man came up to me from the group around the car and chased me away. I ran some distance into the parkland across from the house, found the spot where I had watched from the bushes before, and sat down on the stump. Just as I had then, I kept an eye on Werther's house. But nothing special happened. The bushes were too low to provide enough shelter; once I began getting wet, I made my way home.

Early that same evening, Werther delivered a reply in the form of a letter, which he handed to my mother. She called to me, but by the time I got to the door Werther had disappeared. The letter said: "Dear Elmer. I would like to go with you on Sunday. I will come to your house, you must not come to me. Before Sunday, I will go to your place again. You must not come to my house. Werther." This gave me cause for reflection.

For the rest of the week, he did not show up. I thought he had forgotten all about it, and began a new letter, but destroyed it.

Just before half three on Sunday, having kept a lookout in the attic, I saw Werther coming. We set out. "I'm sure you'll like it," I said, "that's why I'm taking you along." Truth was, I had no desire to go to my aunt and uncle's on my own. They had asked my mother to send me over on this Sunday.

Their home was on the top floor of a building on Tweede Oosterparkstraat. My uncle sold goldfish on the street market and kept his stocks in large tubs on the balcony at the back of the flat. Squatting down, looking at the fish swimming among the floating aquatic plants always made me feel gloomy and aware of desolation drawing near. The house was quite close to the corner of a courtyard, and from the balcony one had a view only of a white-plastered wall. (Wisps of blue smoke often hung over the gardens below.)

During the walk there, we said little. The weather was dark, but dry and without wind. I sensed that the afternoon would end badly.

My aunt greeted us and gave us each a piece of Christmas cake. My uncle was not at home. Sitting down by the window, she took out her zither. Beneath the strings she inserted a trapezoidal piece of sheet

99

music that contained no notes, only dots connected by a jagged line. If the paper was inserted correctly, the dots, each lying beneath a string, indicated the fretting for the melody.

She began, as she always did, with the song about the frog that was eaten by a stork; she sang slowly and loudly.

Werther grinned and stood listening with a foolish expression. I leaned against the door to the alcove.

At the end of a particular verse, the last two words of which were "Sir Stork", I could help myself no longer: my eyes were drawn to the copper vase with peacock feathers on a small, three-legged table beside the door to the alcove. I knew that the great sadness had arrived and I went out onto the balcony. Everything was as I had known it would be. This time, too, a thin veil of smoke hung between the houses. I looked into the tubs, dipped my finger in the water and stared at the blind wall. I knew that I had to go back inside, but also that this would provide no relief.

"That is the wall," I said, "and these are the tubs. The zither is in there, with the song on it. And the peacock feathers are in the vase." I tried to sing this quietly, but it did not help. I went back in through the kitchen; my aunt was still singing the same song. Without turning on the light, I entered the water closet, sat down on the pot and waited. Finally, I got up and remained standing in the hallway, listening. The song was over but the zither, unaccompanied by a voice now, started in on a different tune. I crept soundlessly down the stairs and crossed the street onto the nearby footbridge over the railway. There I remained standing for an hour, watching the smoke from the locomotives blending with the mist. Finally, I came down off the bridge and took up position on the corner, where I could watch the house. That is where I remained waiting, for I had no desire to go up again. After a very long time, Werther came outside.

I followed him for a while, unseen. Then, approaching from behind with great leaps, I frightened him. He was angry at first but did not remain so. "I thought you had gone off somewhere to get something," he said. "Where were you?" "I can't tell you that, not right at this moment," I said, "not even if I wanted to: it simply has to remain a secret." When Werther failed to reply, I said, to fill the silence: "They live in a nasty house, if you ask me. Did you like it up there?" He replied feebly that he had not. We walked on. "We're going to move," he said of a sudden. "To Slingerbeekstraat. That's in the South Plan." I didn't answer him. The move, he volunteered, would take place within the week. He also mentioned the exact address.

I was silent for a long time. Then I said: "You have to be awfully careful when you move house, because there are people who move and then they end up in a house that's not nearly as good as the one they lived in first." After that, neither of us spoke.

"Do you know why I stayed outside?" I asked after a while. "Because this afternoon I think you're boring. You always are, actually." Before he could reply I ran ahead and hid around a corner. From my hiding place I leaped out and frightened him again, but this time I collided with him and caused him to fall. In the course of this, the palms of both his hands were slightly grazed. I apologized and stated that it had been an accident, but in fact I was pleased at having injured him.

From that point on we remained silent as we walked. Werther stared at the ground with a scowl. A number of times I tried to make him laugh, but it was no use. Drawing close to my house, we parted with a murmur.

I never spoke to him after that. Every day after school, though, I walked past his house without ringing the bell.

On the sixth day there were no more curtains at the windows. I went home and found a piece of paper, on which I drew only a few random lines. Then I took my brother's bicycle and rode to Slingerbeekstraat.

It was a bit misty, and the street lights had been lit early. The house number I had committed to memory.

The flat was on the ground floor, close to the corner. The sign with the green star was already affixed to the door.

Without dismounting, I cycled slowly past the windows, then turned and passed again. "It's a dark place, where they live," I said quietly.

At home I lingered about the back garden and pulled the tops off the withered remains of the asters. Then I fetched the hatchet from the attic, to chop thin twigs to pieces on the fence.

Amsterdam, Jan.—Apr. 1949

THE FALL OF THE
BOSLOWITS FAMILY

M Y FIRST ENCOUNTER with the Boslowits family
was at a children's party, a Christmas celebration at the home of friends. On the table lay paper
napkins printed with little green and red festive figures.
A candle was lit at every plate, held upright in a hole
cored from a half-potato which, placed face down, was
wrapped cunningly in matte green paper. The same
decoration had been applied to the flowerpot, which
held the Christmas tree.

Hans Boslowits was sitting close to me, and he held
a slice of bread over the candle flame. "I'm making
toast," he said. There was a boy playing the violin as
well, which almost made me cry, and I thought for a
moment about giving him a kiss. I was seven at the time.

Hans, who was two years older, toyed in seeming
nonchalance with the branches of the Christmas tree,

until one of the candles lit the branch above, causing it to crackle and burst brightly aflame. There was loud shouting, mothers ran up, and all those anywhere near the tree were forced to sit down at the table, or go to the adjoining room, where several fell to playing dominoes on the floor.

Both the brothers Willink were there too, sons of a scholarly couple who made them wear their hair closely shorn, for they felt that an individual's appearance was not of the essence and that in this way cleanliness could most easily be maintained, while no time of value need be spent on combing. The trimming of it their mother did each month with her own clippers, which constituted a considerable monetary saving.

It was wonderful to be around them, for there was nothing they did not dare to do. Some Sundays they came to our house to visit, along with their parents. I would venture out into the neighbourhood with them and toss, as did they, a stone, a rotten potato or a horse's turd into every open window. A delicious fever of friendship liberated me from all fear.

At this particular Christmas party, they entertained themselves by holding a burning candle at an angle above someone's hand or arm, until the hot grease dripped onto the victim's skin and they would leap to their feet with a scream.

Hans Boslowits's mother saw it and said: "I don't think that's nice, not in the slightest." His father smiled, though, because he appreciated the inventiveness and had no need to fear that anyone would play the same trick on him, for he was crippled and paralysed by illness from the waist down. From that evening on, we called them Aunt Jaanne and Uncle Hans.

I greatly longed to observe the crippled man's departure, for I had seen him carried in by two guests, and the sight of it had fascinated me deeply. But when eight thirty came I had no choice but to go home with my parents.

Four days later, still in the midst of the Christmas holidays, I went with my mother to visit the Boslowitses. Their street was laid out around some public gardens, which one had to skirt to get there.

"Well, Master Simon," Uncle Hans said, "Hans is in his room, go on in and play with him." "What are you doing here?" his son asked when I entered. "I've come to play with you, that's what your father said," I answered in bewilderment.

He sported plus fours and a green sweater, wore glasses and a sharp parting in his black hair. I looked around the room and saw, atop the cupboard that housed the fold-down bed, a little statue that when I felt and smelled it turned out to be a dog carved from soap.

"I made that myself," he said. "Did you?" I asked. "At school?" "On my own, at home, with soap from the shop," he claimed, but I no longer believed him, for he had looked confused for a moment by my question.

There was an object on his desk that he examined and handled in a way intended to prompt my utmost curiosity. It was a sort of metal box, two fingers thick and in the form of a writing pad, its lid sloping slightly and with a button on the top. Around the frame was a lid, with a transparent celluloid window in it. One could not only use a pencil, but also a stylus without any ink or lead, or even a twig, to write words on its surface: they appeared in purple at the bottom of the window. If one pushed the button, all one had written vanished.

I had never considered the possibility of something like this existing.

I was given the opportunity to write on it as well and, with a push of the button, to cause the letters to disappear. Sometimes the contraption malfunctioned, however, and the text remained in whole or in part.

"I'm going to throw it away," Hans said, "it's broken." "A nice thing," I said to Aunt Jaanne, who had just come in, "that you can write on and it disappears when you push a button. Hans says he's going to throw it away."

"Now that is really very unkind," Aunt Jaanne said, "he'll throw it away only because he doesn't want to give it away." For the rest of the afternoon I lived in the hope that I might possess the contraption but dared not make any reference to it.

In the living room, too, there were objects of interest to me: an armchair for example, two metres long, upholstered in leather and resting on a round metal base. Due to its fragile construction, I was allowed to slide onto it only from the side, after which I could reach down with my right arm and turn a gear that determined the angle of recline.

On the mantelpiece were two old porcelain plaques with images of an angler and a skater respectively. On the window sill were antique copper buckets containing potted plants: a miniature palm and a number of cacti, including a ball-shaped one covered with fibrous growth which Aunt Jaanne called "the grey-haired plant".

When we sat down at the table for sandwiches, we were given knives with yellow ivory handles. The blades bore a gracefully engraved manufacturer's mark with the letters H.B.L. "What do the letters mean?" I asked, but my mother, Aunt Jaanne and Uncle Hans were so engrossed in conversation that only young Hans heard me.

"The first letter stands for Hans," he said loudly, "and the second for Boslowits." "And the third?" I asked patiently. "But the L," he continued, "ah, the L!" He tapped his fork against the blade. "That is known only to me, my father and a couple of other people." I didn't want to assume the responsibility for asking something that for reasons of importance had to remain a secret, and said nothing.

After the meal came a change. A lady arrived with Hans's brother Otto, about whom my mother had already given me instructions. "Their oldest son is a bit feeble-minded, so don't let me catch you teasing him," she had said.

"Well, here we are again!" the lady shouted and let the boy go like a dog given the liberty to jump up against its master's legs. Otto was bent over as he walked and wore extremely high-soled shoes, the toes of which pointed inwards, and a pair of plus fours like his brother's. His face, strangely contorted with eyes that did not fully match, sweated so profusely that the hairs of his colourless thatch seemed glued to his forehead.

"Well, are you back again, my boy!" his father said. "Yeah," he shouted, "yeah, yeah, Father, Mother!" He kissed them both, Hans as well, and then bounded in place with such force that the whole house shook.

I was startled by the fury of it, but he appeared a gentle enough creature, as my mother had told me.

"Shake hands with Aunt Jet," they commanded him, and after much repeating he was able to utter "Aunt Jet" and "hello, Aunt" until finally they succeeded in getting him to pronounce the combination "Hello, Aunt Jet". "And this is little Simon," Aunt Jaanne said. "Hello, Otto," I said, shaking his soaking-wet hand.

He leaped into the air again and was given something sweet, a bonbon that Aunt Jaanne stuck in his mouth. Whenever someone asked him a question—in the usual fashion, with no answer expected—he would shout "yeah, yeah", "yeah, Mother", unleashing the words in a frenzy.

Someone placed a portable gramophone on the table, and the lady who had arrived with Otto wound the handle.

"He stayed dry last night," the lady said. "Oh, such a big boy, such a big, big boy Otto is," his mother said, "you stayed dry all night, did you now? He's a big boy, isn't he, Sister Annie?"

"Yes, he was a big boy, weren't you, Otto?" the lady said. "So what do you say, then?" his mother asked: "yes, Sister Annie." "Yes Sister Annie," he blurted out as a single word, after much urging.

Otto was busy going through a box of gramophone records. He picked up each one and held it in both hands, right in front of his face, as though smelling it. His nose was red and moist, and at the tip of it was a little yellow pimple.

"He can smell which one it is," explained Uncle Hans, who was in his special chair and helping his son to look. "This one," he said, handing a record to Otto. The boy took it, looked at it, sighed and leaned his elbows on the table for a moment, unfortunately right on top of another record which broke in three with a loud crack. I uttered a groan, but Hans picked up the shatters, looked at the label and said: "It was a really old one, and it was cracked already. It's all right, Otto, my man, it was an old one. An old one, Otto." "Old!" Otto hooted, and placed the record his father had given him on the turntable.

This record was not like the others: it was thin and brown and seemed to be made from cardboard or paper. Only one side was playable. Hans placed a heavy rubber cap over the spindle, for the disc was a bit concave. When it started spinning, a flat voice said: "The Loriton record, which you are hearing now, is suitable for recordings of all types. It is light-weight, flexible and can be played three times as often as a normal gramophone recording."

Then the speaker announced a dance orchestra. When they were finished playing, the voice said: "The Loriton disc is playable on one side only, but if you consult your watch you will see that the playing time is twice that of a shellac disc. And the price, ladies and gentlemen, is no more than the half."

Otto was hopping with impatience. His mother sought out another record right away, this one smaller and with a pink label. Two voices sang the song about the three little tykes.

Through the window I could see a light drizzle falling. Sneaking into Hans's room, I examined the carved dog and toyed with the writing machine, until I was summoned to come along home.

On our way back, I asked my mother: "How old is Otto?" "A bit older than you, mouse," she replied. "But you must be sure never to ask Uncle Hans how old Otto is." Suddenly, the rain seemed to blow a bit harder in our faces.

Sunk in thoughts of my own, I nevertheless heard my mother say: "They are worried that, once they're no longer around, there will be no one to take good care of Otto." Both comments gave me cause for reflection for days to come.

It was only on our second visit that I understood from the conversation that Otto did not live with them, but in a children's home, and that the lady who had brought him that day was from that institution, a nurse with whom Aunt Jaanne was on friendly terms.

It was a Sunday, and so this time my father went along too. As we entered, they were bemoaning Otto's behaviour. Young Hans was at the window, Otto before the antique china cupboard and Uncle Hans was in a chair at the table.

"You see," said Aunt Jaanne as she showed us in, "we were just discussing Otto." "Yeah," Otto shouted, "yeah, Mother!" "There in the office," said Uncle Hans—he was referring to his little study that looked out on the street—"was a plate of grapes. I kept thinking: why is he coming in so often? And each time he had picked a grape from the bunch, and now they are all gone."

Otto laughed and made a little leap in the air. His face shone with sweat. "Mother doesn't think that's very nice at all," Aunt Jaanne said, "you've been very naughty, Otto." "Otto naughty!" the boy shouted, his face contorted in fear.

The gramophone was playing loudly, and the conversation grew even more boisterous when Mr and Mrs Fontein arrived. I had never seen her before, but at home I had heard say that whenever she ran into an acquaintance carrying a shopping bag she would hide in an entranceway, or behind a hedge, so as not to have to greet anyone who went from store to store and bought their own groceries. It was also said of her that when paying an evening visit to friends she would leave for an hour to see if her son, who was nineteen at the time, was sound asleep in bed.

We called her Aunt Ellie, but the grown-ups referred to her in jest as "Crazy Ellie".

My mother had gone to visit her once, but Mrs Fontein admitted her no further than the hallway, saying that she had the pedicurist in at the moment. She did, however, stuff a big bonbon in my mother's mouth with the words: "They're actually more for the upper strata, but I don't begrudge you one."

At home my mother had done a paltry imitation of the voice, sounding more like someone suffering from nasal polyps, but now I was hearing it for real.

Aunt Ellie's husband, my father and Uncle Hans went to the study, the latter moving along in a most singular fashion, bent over with his hands on the backs of the furniture and swinging his thin legs along behind him, haltingly and in turn.

I followed them down the hall and entered the room behind Uncle Hans. "So was that Crazy Ellie?" I asked Uncle Hans, pointing towards the living room. This question, posed as it was in front of the husband, could only have caused him great embarrassment, as I was made to understand later. He dipped into his waistcoat pocket, found a quarter, gave it to me and said: "Now run out and buy yourself an ice cream."

I went outside, where a vendor was passing at that moment, placed the quarter on the cart and said: "An ice waffle." "A five-center?" he asked. "That's fine," I said. "Or a ten-center?" "That's fine, just a waffle," I said. "Five cents or ten cents?" he asked then. No clear decision was made, but he prepared a very big waffle, which was just being handed to me when my mother came out of the house.

"He's been naughty," she told the man, "he was whining for it." I held on to the waffle. My mother pulled me along towards the house. "He's still got change coming!" the vendor shouted, but we were already inside and the door slammed shut behind us. The ice waffle did not appeal to me, and I was allowed to leave it on a saucer in the kitchen.

From that day on the visits became regular, back and forth. On my birthday I received a metal wind-up automobile from my new aunt and uncle, and I did not want them to see that I was actually too big for it.

As a rule, they spent each New Year's Eve with us, and my father would help the cab driver to carry Uncle Hans up the stairs.

The affliction remained unchanged throughout the years, but I remember Aunt Jaanne telling us one afternoon that a recurrent paralysis of the right arm had set in now as well. It was in the year that I first attended a school that prepared its pupils for higher education, and which was located close to the Boslowitses. The

Sunday before the start of the school year, I went to visit them. They asked me to stay for lunch.

Aunt Jaanne was explaining to her sister that they had sent Hans to a boarding school in Laren, for the situation at home had become untenable. "When he argues with his father," she said after we had eaten, and after Uncle Hans had gone to his study, "he pats him on the head, and then his father flies into a terrible rage." She went on to say that a neighbour lady, with whom she had spoken that morning across the garden fence, had more or less reproached her for this decision and said: you already have one child living away from home, and now you send the other boy away too. "I spent the whole morning weeping on the divan," Aunt Jaanne said.

"It was very rude of her to say that," her sister said. "Who does she think she is?" "Tomorrow," I said, "I start school over there"—I pointed in the general direction of the building around the corner—"do you think they'll give me homework on the very first day?"

"Oh no, I don't think they'll do that," Aunt Jaanne said.

Now that young Hans was no longer around I was free to search his room thoroughly, but I found nothing of interest. The little dog was still there, but the writing machine was long gone.

"I was hoping I could borrow a couple of books," I said when Aunt Jaanne came in and found me standing before the bookcase, as though in deepest concentration. "These." More or less at random, I pulled out two volumes of *Bludgeon and Beanstalk*, a children's series about a fat boy and a thin one, and *The Book of Jeremiah, Whose Name was Michiel*. "If Hans would think that's all right," I added. "Well, we think that's all right," Aunt Jaanne said, "because we think you're someone special." "I'll bring them back in good time," I said.

Three years before the war began, they moved to a house with a view of the river, a side-canal and a bare and sandy vacant plot. To get to the house one first had to climb a set of twenty high granite steps. It was there that I watched the big air-defence drills, which were held in what I believe was the autumn of that year.

The Boslowits family had invited any number of friends and acquaintances to watch, and the young people in the crowd climbed through a window at the top of the stairs, above the neighbour's house, and onto the roof. Small formations flew past overhead, and we straddled the ridge at a spot beside the chimney and watched the recoil of the barrels of the anti-aircraft guns on the sandy plot below, which took place each time just before we heard the sound itself. From the roof of a detached town house fifty metres away, machine gunners squeezed off salvo after salvo.

The Willink brothers were there too and tossed pebbles, which they had brought up to the roof with them for this sole purpose, onto the street below. Sirens gave the alarm and the sky grew dark. Then came more squadrons, passing through the little clouds made by the explosions and tossing out green, glowing balls that were extinguished before they reached the ground. The civil defence fire crew turned their hoses on the side-canal and river, to test the equipment. When the din ceased, a hydroplane landed on the river and took off again, barely clearing the big bridge that connects the southern neighbourhoods with the east of the city. I was quite content with the spectacle. We all received a cup of tea with salty, brittle biscuits.

Six months later our family moved to the centre of town, to a house across the river that was no more than a ten-minute walk from the Boslowitses'. More frequent visits were therefore possible. Aunt Jaanne came by even more regularly, and on afternoons when Otto had no school—he was learning to weave mats and string beads somewhere—she would fetch him from the children's home and bring him along for an outing.

That was how, one Friday as I was walking home from the gymnasium, I happened to catch sight of them approaching from the other direction and saw how the boy, more bent over than ever, was leaping like a dancing bear at the end of a chain, so frantically that his mother could barely keep hold of his hand. An eight-year-old neighbour girl from the second floor, who was skipping and had to that end tied one end of the cord to the metal fence before one of the narrow front yards, so that she could swing it with only one hand, intentionally pulled the rope taut in front of Otto's feet at the very moment when he broke free and was allowed to run out ahead to our door. The boy stumbled but did not fall. The girl let go of the rope and ran from Aunt Jaanne, who was almost mute with fury.

I followed them as they climbed the stairs, Aunt Jaanne right behind Otto and still in a flap. Otto leaped across the threshold with a loud thud, in full anticipation of the old picture postcards my mother gave him whenever they visited. "Dear God!" Aunt Jaanne said. "That anyone could do something like that, can you imagine? If I'd caught her, I don't know what I would have done, no." She calmed down a little, yet went on blinking her eyes incessantly, a quirk of hers I noticed then for the first time.

"Let's see if there's a card in here for you," my mother said. "Yeah, Aunt Jet!" Otto bellowed and danced along beside her to the cupboard. There, from a cigar box, she pulled out three cards. He sniffed at them and leaped up high. "Careful, Otto, think of the downstairs neighbours," my mother said.

"And where is Otto going?" Aunt Jaanne asked. "Yeah, yeah, Mother!" "Where are you going?" "Yeah, Mother!" "No, you know, Otto, tell us where you're going." When Otto still gave no satisfactory reply, she said: "To Russia." "To Russia, yeah Mother!" Otto shouted.

"I've been meaning to tell you, Jet," Aunt Jaanne said, "that there is a professor in Russia who has cured a number of children entirely by means of an operation. And ever since we found out about it, he's been talking about Russia."

Her next announcement had to do with Uncle Hans's health. Having suffered a collapse, he now lay in bed and his right arm was almost completely paralysed. "And then his moods on top of it all," she said, "it's something terrible."

By way of encouraging news, she told us that a physician who had treated Uncle Hans ten years ago had recently stopped by to visit them and said: Dear fellow, I thought you'd died a long time ago.

That was not all she had to report, however. They were considering the purchase of an invalid carriage for Uncle Hans, so that, when he was feeling a bit better, he could take more fresh air and visit friends at less expense.

"But he doesn't want that," Aunt Jaanne said. "He thinks it will make him look disabled." "Which is what he is," my mother said.

Despite his objections, Uncle Hans did indeed get a carriage, but only quite some time afterwards. It was a three-wheeler, powered by levers that were used to drive the single front wheel and also to steer.

The carriage could only be kept in a garage for bicycles, which meant Uncle Hans first had to be carried down the flight of stone steps in front of their building. Not so long after he got the carriage, he began renting a ground-floor flat. It was in a dark, damp house on the street behind ours. Yet there were also advantages, for the tenants' council had given permission for the cart to be parked in the entranceway, and a carpenter friend fashioned a letter box that fit in a window of his little study, so the postman could toss his letters almost directly onto his desk.

Yet going out for a spin was, in fact, an autonomous act in name only; someone was always needed to push him: his emaciated hands, in particular the right one, lacked the necessary strength.

One Sunday afternoon my parents and I were returning from a birthday party, along with Otto, Aunt

Jaanne and Uncle Hans, and I pushed the chair along patiently. We crossed a bridge, the approaches to which were very steep.

On the far side of the water, we had to turn left. As we were going down, the chair began rolling faster. I held it in check, but Uncle Hans ordered me to let go. I obeyed. At the bottom of the bridge was a junction, where the presence of a traffic policeman made it impossible to simply swerve off to the left. When the policeman's sign was turned to "go", one had first to cross and then wait one's turn on the right side of the street.

Uncle Hans, however, hurtled down the bridge and across the junction. "You're not allowed!" I shouted after him. Right behind the man with the sign he swerved hard to the left; the extreme velocity and the slope of the approach caused the carriage to tip over and hit the pavement with a crash. The policeman and a number of pedestrians hurried over and righted the chair, with Uncle Hans still in it. He had incurred no injuries, but when we arrived at their house he only sat at the table, staring glumly into space.

Aunt Jaanne did her best to reassure Otto, who she thought had seen the fall and been unsettled by it. "It wasn't Father who fell over, it was some other man, Otto, it was someone else, not Father." "Not Father!" Otto shouted, and leaned his elbow on a teacup, which broke. It was a dark day without rain, but it seemed about to fall at any moment from an impassive sky.

That same spring, on my sixteenth birthday, not only Aunt Jaanne and Uncle Hans came to visit, but young Hans as well. His mother had decided to bring him home again.

"If a war starts, I'd rather have him close by," she said. He was to start work as a salesman in an uncle's business.

"You say 'if a war starts', as though nothing were happening yet," my father said. That was the moment at which the conversation captured my attention. To be sure, Britain and France were at war with Germany, but there were to my disappointment no open hostilities worth mentioning.

Along with Joost, the younger of the Willink brothers, I occasionally visited the cinema, where before the main feature they would show humdrum newsreels from the front, in which camouflaged cannonry stood idle or fired a desultory round every fifteen minutes. Relief from this monotony was found in some footage of the grounded German battleship *Graf von Spee*, magnificently scuttled and broken. "The horrors of war, lovely," Joost said in a comic tone when aerial footage went on to show a general view of the wreck.

"What I'd like most would be violent skirmishes, here in the streets of the city," I said. "Shooting from door to door, with hand grenades and white flags; but only for a day or two, otherwise it starts getting boring."

On an evening in May, when I arrived at the Boslowitses' to borrow a toaster, I found Uncle Hans, Aunt Jaanne and young Hans sitting in the dusk-filled parlour. A neighbour was visiting. They were so engrossed in conversation that, at first, they did not notice me come in.

"What I mean to say," the neighbour was saying, "in other words, is that that means something. It means a great deal more than we know."

After I had stood waiting in the doorway, a bit reticently, Aunt Jaanne caught sight of me. "Oh, it's you," she said. "Have you heard that all military leave has been suspended? This gentleman's son has to report back this evening already, he has to be back in the barracks tonight."

"No," I said, "is that right?" "It's been on the radio," the neighbour said.

"Then something's afoot, in any case," I said, and felt a deep thrill rise up inside me.

That same week, a few hours past midnight on the Friday morning, virtually the entire neighbourhood gathered outside in the street. Planes were droning past overhead, anti-aircraft guns roared and searchlights poked their shafts between the thin wisps of cloud.

"They'll be getting the brunt of it again, over there in England," a milkman said, for he had deduced that these planes now being fired upon by our neutral forces above Dutch territory were German ones, on their way to English cities.

As far as the planes' provenance went, he was proven right; the rest of his hypothesis was refuted, however, once we realized the import of the deep thundering and play of lights on the south-western horizon.

At a little past seven that morning, Aunt Jaanne came up the stairs to our house. I was not at home, for the Willink brothers had come with their sister to fetch me. From the balcony of their home, I could see heavy clouds hanging over a spot that could only be the airfield at Schiphol.

"It's war," said their sister, whose name was Lies. Elated by so many fascinating events at one and the same time, the four of us returned to my house. It was a quarter to eight.

"It's war," my mother said, "they said so on the radio." "What exactly did they say?" I asked. "Oh, I can't repeat it word for word, you should have listened to it yourself," she said.

Aunt Jaanne, wearing a black velveteen cap, was sitting in the armchair and blinking her eyes. The radio was silent at that moment, and we waited impatiently for the eight o'clock news broadcast to begin. Custom had it that this was heralded by the crowing of a cock.

"I'm curious whether they'll start off today with the old cock-a-doodle-doo," said my father, coming in from the hall.

I hoped desperately that all the rumours flying around the neighbourhood were true. "Really, truly at war, glorious," I said under my breath.

The broadcaster's clock began to make the slight grating sound that preceded the striking of the hour. After the sixteen notes of the introductory tune, the strokes rang out, slow and clear. Then the cock crowed. "Scandalous, that's what it is," my father said.

I was startled, for this meant everything might be ruined now. This was most likely an indication that war had not broken out at all. Only when the reader announced the crossing of the borders of the Netherlands, Belgium and Luxembourg by German troops did I feel reassured.

I left contentedly for school that morning, while Aunt Jaanne still sat in our armchair, staring into space without a word.

The mood at school was solemn. The building, the

headmaster announced in the big assembly hall, was going to be used as a field hospital. After his address, we all sang the national anthem. The fact that the school would be closed for the time being made the day even more invigorating, as though all things had become new.

It was not until late that Tuesday afternoon that we saw Aunt Jaanne again. She came to visit on her own and looked pale.

"What are you people doing?" she asked. "Is something burning? What's that stench? It's all quite beastly, isn't it?"

"Beastly is the word for it," my mother said. "They've just announced the surrender." We were burning books and pamphlets in the stove which, stuffed as it was with paper, had begun to smoke and draw poorly. My father and brother had meanwhile begun to fill two gunny sacks and a suitcase with books. After dark, they tossed them into the canal.

There were fires all over the neighbourhood that evening, with new fuel brought in all the time, sometimes by the crateful. Many people, too, tossed everything into the water. In their haste, they sometimes left things lying on the quay. That evening, strolling along the waterfront, I found a book bound in bright red, the title of which I've forgotten but which my mother took from my room and refused to give back.

After being told of the capitulation, the news of which she asked my mother to repeat again, Aunt Jaanne suddenly stood up and left. The next day brought two events of interest. Early in the afternoon, the first Germans entered the city: motorcyclists in green, mottled coats. A few civilians loitered at the kerbside to watch them cross the bridge. Aunt Jaanne had seen them too and, when she visited us on Wednesday evening, she referred to them as frogs.

I was not at home when she came, for I was busy. A mistake had been made, people said, and salt water had been let into the polder waterways; hundreds of fish were floating to the surface, gasping for oxygen. Using a large landing net, I collected them to take home; they made no attempt to get away, and I was able to bring home a whole pailful.

Classes resumed the next day; to console myself, I went that first evening to a little cinema where a French film, *Hotel North*, was being shown that week for the last time. It was about a suicide pact in which the boy shot the girl, but then lacked the courage to turn the gun on himself. The girl recovered, however, and the film ended with them being reconciled and at peace with life, after she had fetched him from the prison gates. It was a resolution that left me satisfied.

At home I found Aunt Jaanne sitting on the divan, with my mother pouring coffee for the two of them.

The room was dim, as no lights had been turned on as yet; rolling down the paper blackout curtains and tacking them into place was a tiresome task. That is how I found them, by the sombre glow of a tea light.

"You need to black out the room," I said. "You can see that candlelight all the way outside."

"You do it, would you?" my mother said.

As I unfurled the black rolls, I remember noticing that one of the windows was open a crack. "Hans sent a letter to his aunt in Berlin," Aunt Jaanne said, "a long time ago. It came back, marked undeliverable. 'No longer at this address, new address unknown', the envelope said."

At that moment a gust of wind rushed in, lifting the blackout paper and the curtain for a second and knocking a sheet of paper off the table. I quickly closed the window.

At the end of one of my afternoons off, I stopped by to see the Boslowitses. The weather had turned to high summer, and Uncle Hans was sitting in the sun at the window of his study.

He quickly brought the conversation round to his illness, and to the doctor, Witvis by name, who had now been to see him several times and planned to do something to cure him. "What he really needs to do is make me able to run," he said, "like a rabbit. I bet you're dying for a cigarette, aren't you?" he asked, and got up to look for the case. "If you tell me where they are, I'll fetch them," I said, but he had already shuffled to one corner of the room, where he took a shallow copper case from the table. "Are you laughing?" he asked, his back still turned to me. "Absolutely not," I said.

Young Hans came in and sat down on the corner of his father's desk. "How are things with you?" I asked. "Do you enjoy sales?" "Today I raked in about a thousand guilders," he replied.

"Is there any news?" Aunt Jaanne asked. "News is," I replied, "that the Germans are advancing on Brest, they're making a huge to-do about it on the radio." Then I related the claim I'd heard made by a fat boy in my class. According to a prediction made by a French priest some forty years ago, the Germans would be defeated at Orleans. "'The city on the Meuse shall be destroyed,' he wrote that too," I said. "If you bring me the book with that in it, I'll give you a reward," Aunt Jaanne said.

That same afternoon, just before dinner, I stopped by the Willinks' to bring them the latest news. I had barely settled down in Eric's room when the anti-aircraft guns began thudding restlessly. Two machines were flying overhead, so high that that one could perceive only the reflection of sunlight, but not their shapes.

A little later came the rattle of machine guns and the terrific roar of a warplane low over our heads. Every time the noise grew too loud, we raced back inside from the balcony; we could hear the thumping of the auto-cannons as well.

When the guns fell silent for a moment, we saw a black smudge in the sky, and at the tip of it a fiery star falling fast. Its light was as white as the glow made by the electric welding of metal. Then we saw a second column of smoke rising from the comet: the aircraft had broken in two.

Within an instant, the whole scene had disappeared behind the rooftops. There was no parachute in sight against the sky. "God be with those who move upon the sea or in the air," I said solemnly. No air raid siren had sounded.

After dinner, Hans Boslowits came to our house. "Do you know what kind of plane it was?" he asked. "No, I don't," I replied. "It was German," he stated. "How can you be sure?" I asked. "Have you heard where it came down?"

"Listen," Hans said, cleaning his spectacles with his handkerchief, "we have our sources."

"I certainly hope that's true," I said, "but I don't believe one could know that yet for a certainty." "We have our sources," he said, and left.

Coming back from the cinema the next day, I believe it was a weekday, I saw the news of the French surrender posted outside the offices of a newspaper. "What they're asking for is truce," my mother said at home, when I told her about the late edition. "That's not the same thing. Go tell the Boslowitses exactly that."

"It could be simply propaganda," Aunt Jaanne said when I got there, but it was clear to me that she never doubted the report for a moment. She came to our house that same evening; it was only then that she told us what had happened to her a good four weeks earlier.

Of an afternoon, two uniformed Germans had arrived in a car. "Don't move," one of them had shouted as he entered Uncle Hans's study. "You must be joking, man," Uncle Hans replied in German. "I can't even stand on my own two feet."

After searching the house, they announced that he was to come with them. Uncle Hans went to get dressed, but when they saw him dragging himself around the house in his partial paralysis, they realized how senseless it would be to arrest him.

They also watched as Aunt Jaanne bound a rubber flask to the front of him, to urinate into. "They asked me whether I was the only one who knew how to do that," she said. "I told them I was. They took a few notes and then they just went away, but it was quite unnerving." She was blinking rapidly again and the muscles in her face were beset by little tremors.

"And how is Hans getting along otherwise?" my mother asked. "Well, he's not getting any worse," Aunt Jaanne said, "in fact, he's able to use that hand to write with again, for the moment at least." "Well, you see, there you go," my mother said.

The summer and the autumn passed dismally. After New Year the weather was mild and moist. On the second Sunday of the new year I was invited to dinner by the parents of my schoolmate Jim, where I unexpectedly found young Hans as well.

Jim's father was a wholesaler in veal and had an enormously fat belly, yet he was a cheerful man and took things as they came. He had already had three stomach operations, but he denied himself nothing.

"I'll eat anything," he said at the table, "as long as it doesn't have pins in it." In all cordiality, they had invited my parents to accompany me and become acquainted too.

"I've stopped reading German books," said a little grey-haired man at the table when the subject of literature was brought up. This immediately led to a discussion of the war, and both guests and hosts did their best to estimate how long it would last. "I would say," Jim's father stated, "that it will be six months at the very most, but it will never last that long."

"The way things are going at the moment," my father said with a smile, "it might last twenty-five years."

Hans, who turned out to be an acquaintance of one of Jim's brothers, had brought along his guitar and loudly played a popular number of the day, 'Skating over the Rainbow'. When the war came up, he said: "It will be over before the end of the year." "What makes you think that, Hans?" my mother asked. "The sources who provide me with information, Aunt Jet," he replied, "are very well, I repeat, very well informed."

About six weeks later Aunt Jaanne climbed the stairs to our house in a state of great agitation. "The military police are picking up all the young men around Waterlooplein," she said. "Could little Simon go and take a look for me? No, wait, better if he goes straight to Hans's office, to warn him not to go out on the street. Hold on, I'll call him first. Ask Simon to wait, would you?"

"Sit down for a moment first, Jaanne" my mother said. We succeeded in calming her. It was a Wednesday afternoon. "Now why don't you try giving young Hans a call?" my mother said. "I've already done that," said

Aunt Jaanne. "Well there, you see," said my mother. "I don't mind at all, really, I'll go down and take a look," I announced. "As long as you are very, very careful," was my mother's admonishment.

I cycled quickly to the neighbourhood around Waterlooplein, and upon returning to the Boslowitses' reported everything with care. Uncle Hans was puffing slowly on his short black pipe. "That's a nice sweater you've got there," he said suddenly, in the midst of my account. "Is it new?" Aunt Jaanne was on the phone the whole time, talking to the people in the office where young Hans worked. He was going to spend the night there: I heard her promise to have bedclothes and food brought to him. At her request, I took the receiver. "Don't believe for a moment that what you've said, most respected Simon of mine, means anything at all," I heard the voice at the other end say. "Well, well," I answered, smiling, for Aunt Jaanne was keeping a close eye on me. "That woman makes such a terrible fuss," he went on, "tell her I said she's a horrible old nag." The connection was extraordinarily clear, so I tapped my left foot noisily on the floor by way of disguise. "Yes, of course," I said loudly, "I can imagine that quite easily, very good." "What are you talking about?" he asked. "Exactly that, that you'll be careful, but I know you will. Bye! See you soon!" and I placed the receiver back on the hook, ignoring young Hans's furious screams, which produced whistling sounds on the line.

"Well then, what did he say?" Aunt Jaanne asked. "He says," I affirmed, "that we are all nervous and that we're telling each other silly stories. But you absolutely mustn't worry, he says. He wouldn't dream of going outside. But it will all be over in a day, he says."

"I may ask you to phone again later," Aunt Jaanne said contentedly. Then, looking out of the window, she murmured: "Not to worry, don't be silly."

Four days later Aunt Jaanne came to the house looking for my mother, who was off visiting acquaintances but expected to return any moment. While she waited, the fat magician who lived around the corner came up the central staircase. As always, as he climbed he whistled the melody that preceded the London broadcasts. "You shouldn't whistle on the stairs like that," I told him. "It doesn't do anyone any good, and it's dangerous." After hearing the dismal news, he said: "I do believe they're going to lose this war, although I don't know if that will be before or after my funeral." Then he left our house again, shaking with laughter and whistling the same melody loudly as he went down the stairs. He had barely gone when my mother returned.

"The Parkman girl is dead," Aunt Jaanne said once my mother arrived. She told us how the daughter of the man across the street had taken poison, along with her husband. The man had been brought around in the hospital and was already recovering. "He keeps screaming, and they have to restrain him," Aunt Jaanne said. "Who's she talking about, the father or the son-in-law?" I wondered.

The month of June was balmy, a splendid patch of early summer. On an afternoon when my mother was knitting by the open window, Aunt Jaanne came by with Otto. She was pale, and the skin on her face looked dry and chalky, even though she used no powder. "Mother, Mother!" Otto shouted impatiently. "Yes, you're a sweet boy, now be quiet for a moment, darling," Aunt Jaanne said.

She had come to tell us about something that had happened to one of her nephews. While cycling through the centre of town he had committed a traffic offence and was detained by a man, wearing half civilian clothes and half in uniform, with black boots, who grinned as he wrote down the young man's name.

One evening, a few days later, a darkly dressed man knocked on their door, keeping to the shadows the whole time and saying that the nephew was to report to a certain office the next afternoon to, as the man put it, set things right with regard to a traffic offence.

He went, but his mother went with him. At the entrance to the office in question she was held back, while her son was allowed to go in. Twenty minutes later he stumbled back out, gagging, with several bruises and bleeding wounds on his head and his clothes all dusty, as though they had been dragged over the ground.

For a considerable sum, they were able to hire a coach with pneumatic tyres, drawn by a pony, to take them home. When the doctor arrived, he said the boy not only had a minor concussion and bruises to the left shoulder, but that the collarbone on that side was fractured as well.

First, the young man said, they had made him wait in a little room. The man who had detained him on the street came in first, then fetched a few others, some of whom carried rubber truncheons. "This is that cheeky little fellow who thought he could call me a bastard," he announced. One of the other men struck him a blow to the chin, then all six or seven of them suddenly began punching and kicking.

"It started just like that," the boy told Aunt Jaanne. A man with greasy grey hair had repeatedly tried to kick him in the stomach. While dodging the blows, the boy tripped and fell on his back. Before he could protect himself, one of the men stomped on his chest. After he rolled over, the grey man, he thought it was, had jumped with both feet on his back.

Then an alarm or a whistle sounded, in any case a high-pitched sound that caused them all to stop; at that point he heard a crowd of voices but could remember nothing beyond that, until he got outside.

"Have you heard already," Aunt Jaanne asked then, "about Jozef? His people received notification that he was dead." "No," my mother said, "I didn't know that." "The peculiar thing, though, is that on the same day they also received a letter from him, from the camp," Aunt Jaanne went on, "with a much later date on it. And now they've stopped hearing anything at all."

No one spoke a word. Aunt Jaanne looked at Otto and said: "The doctor has given him powders; for the last two nights he's stayed dry, that's what the nurse told me." Realizing that she had forgotten to give Otto his postcards, my mother took two out of the cupboard: one was of a brightly coloured foreign cityscape against a pink sky.

When I came to visit him a few weeks later, young Hans was playing his guitar. He strummed with his whole hand and bounced his foot up and down as he played. At my request he played 'O Jozef, Jozef', but the rendition failed to please me, for he followed the melody by singing a chorus of "ta ta ta ta" all too emphatically, stretching the tendons in his neck to make his voice rasp in a silly way.

"The heartbeat of our society, that music is," he said. At that moment there was a knock at the little window in the front door. The visitor had already entered the hallway, and Aunt Jaanne cried out: "It's all right, it's only the neighbour, come on in."

"I dropped by to tell you, because I'm sure you haven't heard yet, Mrs Boslowits," the neighbour said as he came into the room. "But Dr Witvis is dead."

"How can that be?" Aunt Jaanne asked. "I just heard about it," he said, "it happened only last night."

Late in the evening, he told us, the doctor had taken a razor and cut the wrists of his two young sons, after which he held their forearms in a bath of warm water to eliminate the pain. After his wife had opened her veins, he cut his own wrist in the same fashion. This series of events had been reconstructed from the positions in which the victims were found, and the presence of a second razor in the wife's hand. The wife and children were dead when they found them, the father was unconscious. After the wound had been sealed and bound, he was taken to hospital and given transfusions, but he died before noon without ever coming to.

In late autumn, when I went to the Boslowitses' one Sunday afternoon to borrow half a loaf of bread, I found Otto standing beside the gramophone.

"Otto's taking a trip," Aunt Jaanne said, "aren't you, Otto?" "Yes, Mother," the boy shouted, "Otto taking trip!" "Where on earth is he going?" I asked.

Aunt Jaanne's face looked as though she were flushed with fever. "He can't stay at the children's home and the school any more," she told me, "he has to go to Apeldoorn. I'm taking him there tomorrow."

Only then did I see that the sliding doors were open to the back bedroom, where Uncle Hans was lying in bed. The bed frame with its white iron bars had ornamental copper balls at all four corners. The sick man's face was thin, yet seemed swollen as well, as though it were wet on the inside.

On a chair beside him were vials of medicine, a breakfast plate with a knife, and a chessboard. "Hans and I were playing chess earlier this afternoon," he said, "but Otto kept knocking it over."

In the days that followed, he remained in bed and his condition worsened. Winter was coming and the new doctor ordered them to turn up the heating throughout the house. For a time, Uncle Hans was able to reach the water closet under his own power, but eventually he had to be helped.

"The man is so incredibly heavy, I can't do it on my own," Aunt Jaanne said. "And what's more, he puts up a fight."

In early January, the doctor recommended that he be urgently admitted to hospital, where he was taken at the beginning of that same week.

"He's truly in excellent hands there," Aunt Jaanne told my mother at the end of one of her visits. "The doctors and the nurses, they're all so very kind."

"He's lost touch completely, though," she went on, "I don't understand what gets into that man. Hans brought him some oranges: he was able to buy them through someone at the office. He tells him: Father, these oranges cost sixty cents apiece, be sure you eat them all. But he didn't eat a single one, he gave them all away. It's only natural that one should share, but that is infuriating."

One day in early summer, Aunt Jaanne said to my mother: "Starting tomorrow we have to be inside by eight. Do you think you could go to the hospital to visit him in the evenings? I wouldn't have enough time to get back, and what good would it do Hans if I were to leave again after only three minutes? I'll just stay a little longer during the day, they won't mind."

The evening after she had visited the hospital for the first time, my mother reported to Aunt Jaanne at their house. "He looks good, he seems to be putting on weight," she said. Aunt Jaanne, however, seemed barely to hear. Young Hans had not yet come home, and she asked my mother to call his office from another phone, for theirs had recently been disconnected. "Have little Simon go to the office and see if he's still there." My mother was just about to carry out her request when Hans came in the door.

The streets had been barricaded, but the people at the office were warned beforehand. He left once the way seemed clear, but halfway home he'd had to hide in a public urinal. When eight o'clock came he sprinted the final stretch, through our neighbourhood.

"We're not allowed to leave town any more," Aunt Jaanne told me one evening, when I arrived to say that my mother had a previous engagement and would not be able to visit Uncle Hans that next Friday. "Be a dear and ask your mother if she'll go to visit Otto this week."

The next day, a Wednesday afternoon, Aunt Jaanne came to our house. "They're taking inventories," she said. When my mother invited her to sit down and poured her a cup of apple tea, she told us that everyone else in their building had received a visit from the auditors, two men with briefcases. They had searched the houses and noted anything of value. On their way out, they came across the five-year-old son of the second-floor neighbours, playing with a little dark-red wallet on the stairs.

One of the men took it from him, opened it and took out a nickel five-cent piece and three little silver coins, then gave it back. "That one isn't really a quarter," the child said, "it's something from way back, that's what my father says." "You just keep nice and quiet, little boy," the man had told him, "you just keep very nice and quiet."

Aunt Jaanne did not know whether she had simply failed to hear them knocking; in any case, they had left without searching her house.

She asked me to go along right away and had me carry off, packed in a suitcase, a Frisian clock, some antique porcelain, two carved ivory candlesticks and the two old porcelain plaques. I brought it all home and went back twice more to fetch some decorative plates, a camera and a lovely little mirror.

Once every two weeks, usually on a Tuesday, my mother went to Apeldoorn to visit Otto in the big institution there. When she came home in the afternoon, that first time, Aunt Jaanne was waiting for her. "How was it?" she asked. "He looks quite well," my mother said, "and he was so happy to see me. The nurses are all so nice to him."

"Didn't he ask about home?" Aunt Jaanne asked. "No, not once," my mother said, "and he played nicely with all the other children. When I left he looked sad for a moment, but I wouldn't say he missed anything, no, not that."

She provided her with a detailed description of how she was received by the nurse in the ward; how she had given her the sweets to pass out to the children, but had kept aside a bag of cherries, to give to Otto during their walk in the sun along a forest path.

"I would feed him some from time to time," she said, "but he preferred to take them out of the bag himself. I was afraid he might get some of the juice on his clothes, but he was really quite good about that."

Later on, once Aunt Jaanne had left, she told me that the boy had been sloppily dressed and that his trousers were held up with a length of cord, rather than with a belt or braces. "And his shoes," she said, "fit him so badly, I don't understand how they can let them wear such idiotic things. They're understaffed, of course, the people there do all they can."

She also described to me how Otto had said a few times: "To Mother." "Mother's at home, she'll come sometime soon," she told him. "Mother home," he had shouted then. When she left at the end of the afternoon, he had wept.

A week later, right after dinner, Aunt Jaanne appeared at our door. "They've started," she said, "they're rounding people up. No more notice, they're picking them up just like that. They took the Allegros. Do you know them?" "No, I've never met them," my mother said.

Aunt Jaanne asked me to go right away to the hospital with a letter and ask for an affidavit saying that Uncle Hans was seriously ill. I went, and at the main entrance was referred to an office in one of the wards, where I handed in the letter. Ten minutes later, I was given a sealed white envelope, which I took to Aunt Jaanne.

The next evening, she came back. She asked me to go again. "It says that he is seriously ill, but that should be: mortally ill," she said. "I don't know if they're going to want to put that in writing," I said, "but we'll see."

The head nurse read Aunt Jaanne's note and the first affidavit; after a fifteen-minute wait, she handed me a new envelope.

"You know, Simon," Aunt Jaanne said two days later, "I need you to go again and ask them to draw up a new affidavit, stating the nature of his illness. The nature of it. Not in Latin, but perhaps in German, so it's easier to understand."

She gave me the most recent affidavit, but no note this time to go with it. I returned to the hospital.

"Mrs Boslowits asks whether you could please include the nature of the illness," I said. "Preferably not in Latin." The head nurse took the envelope and came back a little later. "Could I ask you to wait for a bit?" she asked. After a time, I was given an identical sealed envelope.

I brought it to the Boslowitses' right away and found Aunt Jaanne and young Hans sitting at the window. The room was almost dark. The drapes were open, the lace curtains had been slid aside and from the bay window she and Hans had a view of the street.

"There we are, that's fine," Aunt Jaanne said after reading the statement. "Do you really believe that it's going to make the slightest difference?" said Hans. "Indeed," I replied. "He knows, he knows," I said, under my breath. "What did you say?" Aunt Jaanne asked. "I was humming," I said.

Not only my mother, but also other of the Boslowitses' acquaintances who visited them after dark spoke in sombre amazement of the situation in their home. "It's like a haunted house," my mother said.

I visited them regularly in the evening too, and each time it was the same. The ringing of the bell, the turning of the deadlock, and by the time I reached the hall Aunt Jaanne would already have gone back inside. When I entered the living room she would be sitting at the window on the left side of the bay, young Hans at the right. As soon as I was inside, Aunt Jaanne would leave her post for a moment, hurry into the hallway and lock the front door. When I left, she would walk with me and lock it behind me. Back out on the street I could see them again, already sitting at the window like statues. I would wave, but they never responded.

One Tuesday morning, their neighbours came to tell us that two policemen in black helmets had come to the Boslowitses' home at eight thirty the previous evening. Aunt Jaanne had shown them the affidavit from the hospital, which one of them had inspected by the light of a pocket torch. "And who are you?" he asked young Hans. When he told him, the other policeman said: "He's not on the list." "Come with us, the two of you," the first one said.

When friends told Uncle Hans what had happened, he said nothing. They thought he had not heard them or had not understood and repeated it a few times with emphasis. He tried to sit up straight, then, after someone had slid a few pillows behind his back, he sat and stared out of the window. The visitors, a lady friend of Aunt Jaanne's and her daughter, had finally left and gone home.

On a certain day, a neighbour lady knocked on our door. "They're emptying out the infirmary," she said.

She had watched as hundreds of elderly people were carried down the steps and loaded into waiting vehicles, and heard a ninety-two-year-old man, who looked rather familiar to her, shout: "I'm being borne up on the wings of an eagle!"

"The mental institution at the Apeldoornse Bos was emptied out yesterday too," she said.

"What did you tell him about Otto?" I asked my mother, the next time she returned from visiting Uncle Hans. "The way things are, that it's all been evacuated," she said. "He says he only hopes the boy was killed right away. The doctors and nurses stayed with the patients, did you know that?" "No," I said, "I didn't."

Early the next week, one of Uncle Hans's friends hired a carriage and transferred him from the hospital to an attic room in the centre of the city, which an acquaintance had allowed them to do up for that purpose. Late in the evening, he also fetched the invalid carriage—its tyres had already been stolen—from the entranceway of Uncle Hans's house. Within a few days, the house was stripped bare, but they agreed to keep that news from Uncle Hans for the time being.

The sick man lay alone in his new quarters, but a nurse came twice a day to care for him. Very few knew of his whereabouts.

During the summer, everything went as well as one could hope. When autumn came, however, new lodgings had to be found for Uncle Hans, because no stove could be lit in the attic room.

They succeeded in finding a place for him in a home for the elderly. The paperwork would be taken care of.

When they informed him of the decision, he was disappointed. He stated that he would rather be lodged with friends.

Sometimes he seemed not to know what he was saying; one afternoon he said to the nurse: "You remember, don't you, when I was twenty-seven? No, I mean in 1927, I remember it clearly, so—" and then he lay there, lost in thought.

One Wednesday he received a visit from a female acquaintance, an artist. "You always did admire that atlas, didn't you?" he asked. "Come now, be truthful." Uncle Hans owned an atlas with maps of the world, which was considered very authoritative and valuable and which friends had taken to safety from his house.

When the nurse arrived that afternoon, he said: "Bring that atlas along next time, would you? I'm going to give it to Ali." "That's silly," she said, "it's much too lovely to just give away." "No, bring it along, I'm telling you," he said, and asked her for something to drink.

The next day, the daughter of Aunt Jaanne's lady friend came by and found him asleep. "He's sleeping," she told them when she came home. That evening the nurse arrived, found him resting, took his pulse and left without concern. The next morning, when she arrived at the usual hour, she found him cold. She lifted his head; the little hair still on it felt wet. The thin lips were closed, the spectacles lent him an air of the unreal.

"It didn't sink in right away," she said later, "and then I thought I heard something peculiar, but it was only a vacuum cleaner on the ground floor."

When she saw the empty pillbox beside the drained glass, it dawned on her. Counting back, however, she realized that it could have contained no more than four sleeping tablets. The only possible conclusion was that he had been stowing them away regularly, to accumulate a supply.

At night, the friend who had fetched him from the hospital, along with the man whose room it was, carried the corpse down the stairs and lowered it on a rope into the nearby canal, where it sank without a sound, or so I am told.

The two men then hurried back to the house, where they waited with the nurse until four in the morning before returning home.

Until that hour, they spoke of all manner of things: the distances between the planets, the probable duration of the war and the existence or absence of a God. Both men also took note of the nurse's words, when she told them that Uncle Hans had had enough money to keep him alive for another year. "That was not the reason why," she said.

══

THE SPECTRE OF ALEXANDER WOLF

GAITO GAZDANOV

'A mesmerising work of literature' Antony Beevor

SUMMER BEFORE THE DARK

VOLKER WEIDERMANN

'For such a slim book to convey with such poignancy the extinction of a generation of "Great Europeans" is a triumph' *Sunday Telegraph*

MESSAGES FROM A LOST WORLD

STEFAN ZWEIG

'At a time of monetary crisis and political disorder... Zweig's celebration of the brotherhood of peoples reminds us that there is another way' *The Nation*

THE EVENINGS

GERARD REVE

'Not only a masterpiece but a cornerstone manqué of modern European literature' Tim Parks, *Guardian*

BINOCULAR VISION

EDITH PEARLMAN

'A genius of the short story' Mark Lawson, *Guardian*

IN THE BEGINNING WAS THE SEA

TOMÁS GONZÁLEZ

'Smoothly intriguing narrative, with its touches of sinister,
Patricia Highsmith-like menace' *Irish Times*

BEWARE OF PITY

STEFAN ZWEIG

'Zweig's fictional masterpiece' *Guardian*

THE ENCOUNTER

PETRU POPESCU

'A book that suggests new ways of looking at the world
and our place within it' *Sunday Telegraph*

WAKE UP, SIR!

JONATHAN AMES

'The novel is extremely funny but it is also sad and
poignant, and almost incredibly clever' *Guardian*

THE WORLD OF YESTERDAY

STEFAN ZWEIG

'*The World of Yesterday* is one of the greatest memoirs of the twentieth
century, as perfect in its evocation of the world Zweig loved, as it is
in its portrayal of how that world was destroyed' David Hare

WAKING LIONS

AYELET GUNDAR–GOSHEN

'A literary thriller that is used as a vehicle to explore big
moral issues. I loved everything about it' *Daily Mail*

FOR A LITTLE WHILE

RICK BASS

'Bass is, hands down, a master of the short form, creating in a few pages
a natural world of mythic proportions' *New York Times Book Review*

JOURNEY BY MOONLIGHT
ANTAL SZERB

'Just divine... makes you imagine the author has had private access to your own soul' Nicholas Lezard, *Guardian*

BEFORE THE FEAST
SAŠA STANIŠIĆ

'Exceptional... cleverly done, and so mesmerising from the off... thought-provoking and energetic' *Big Issue*

A SIMPLE STORY
LEILA GUERRIERO

'An epic of noble proportions... [Guerriero] is a mistress of the telling phrase or the revealing detail' *Spectator*

FORTUNES OF FRANCE
ROBERT MERLE

1 *The Brethren*
2 *City of Wisdom and Blood*
3 *Heretic Dawn*

'Swashbuckling historical fiction' *Guardian*

TRAVELLER OF THE CENTURY
ANDRÉS NEUMAN

'A beautiful, accomplished novel: as ambitious as it is generous, as moving as it is smart' Juan Gabriel Vásquez, *Guardian*

A WORLD GONE MAD
ASTRID LINDGREN

'A remarkable portrait of domestic life in a country maintaining a fragile peace while war raged all around' *New Statesman*

MIRROR, SHOULDER, SIGNAL
DORTHE NORS

'Dorthe Nors is fantastic!' Junot Díaz

RED LOVE: THE STORY OF AN EAST GERMAN FAMILY
MAXIM LEO

'Beautiful and supremely touching... an unbearably poignant description of a world that no longer exists' *Sunday Telegraph*